TALES FROM THE BASOTHO

Publications of the American Folklore Society
MEMOIR SERIES
Wm. Hugh Jansen, General Editor
Volume 59   1974

Tales from the Basotho

MINNIE POSTMA

translated from Afrikaans by Susie McDermid

analytical notes, tale type and motif indexes by John M. Vlach

PUBLISHED FOR THE *American Folklore Society* BY THE
UNIVERSITY OF TEXAS PRESS, AUSTIN & LONDON

Translated from *Litšōmo*
Copyright © 1964 by Afrikaanse Pers-Boekhandel
Copyright © 1974 by the American Folklore Society
All Rights Reserved

Library of Congress Cataloging in Publication Data

Postma, Minnie, comp.
  Tales from the Basotho.

  (Publications of the American Folklore Society.
Memoir Series, v. 59)
  Translation of Litsomo.
  CONTENTS: The giant bird Mothemelle.—Wolf and
Jakal and the beautiful girl.—The outcast [etc.]
  1. Tales, Basuto. I. Title. II. Series:
American Folklore Society. Memoirs, v. 59
GR360.B3P613   398.2'0968'6   73–17434
ISBN O–292–74608–3

Composition and printing by The University of Texas Printing Division, Austin
Binding by Universal Bookbindery, Inc., San Antonio

To my first editor and friend,
JAN J. VAN SCHAIK

CONTENTS

Foreword   xi

Translator's Introduction   xv

THE TALES

1. The Giant Bird Mothemelle   3
2. Wolf and Jackal and the Beautiful Girl   12
3. The Outcast   17
4. Fenya-fenyane   23
5. Hen, Hawk, and the Needle   37
6. Roaqo, the Woman Who Ate People   42
7. Tortoise and Dove   50
8. The Guilty Woman   53
9. Monyohe, the Great Snake of the Deep Waters . .   58
10. Maliane and the Water Snake   71
11. Molaetsane   78
12. Obe, the Monster of the Dark Canyon   84
13. The Dove, the Heron, and Jackal   92
14. The Mother-in-Law and the Clear Water . . .   96
15. The Milk Tree   105
16. Jackal and Hen   115
17. The Whirlwind and the Land of the Half-men . .   118
18. Nanabolele, Who Shines in the Night   124

19. Sheep and Baboon 132
20. The Woman with the Big Thumbnail 136
21. Tsananapa 142
22. Masilo, Masilonyane, and the Old Woman . . . 146
23. The Bride of Chief Bulane 152

Appendix: Index of motifs, of tale types, and comparable .
    African folktales 165
Bibliography 175

FOREWORD

No doubt some members of the American Folklore Society will be a little startled to find this volume one of their Memoirs in an era when publishers ignore collectanea and are dedicated to issuing interlinear (and painful) texts. In the selection process of a jury of readers—a process to which this editor is unwaveringly devoted and with which he complies even when its verdict disagrees with his own, although this time it did not disagree with him and he is more devoted than ever—the first reader to appraise the manuscript was quite negative, dismissing the work as *cute*, hardly a term to warrant scholarly publication; the second was neutral, less than enthusiastic, because of the lack of Sesotho texts; but then three quite affirmative votes came from readers who were an Africanist, an African folklorist, and an American folklorist.

I hope the doubting members will read through the volume; I feel confident that, if they do read, the majority of them will agree with me that this is a rare and excellent work. For the lay reader the volume, I think, will present a certain charm and a challenge to see the other-than-simple narrative significance: for instance, the sophisticated interplay of two proverbs in story 19; the flight from the female cannibal in 20, which has so many parallels including the American Negro version in the Alabama Federal Writers' Project in Ben Botkin's *Treasury of American Folklore* (pp. 682–687);

the jealousy in 21 like that of Joseph's brethren in the Old Testament; and 22 with its reminiscences of Cain and Abel combined with the common motif of the singing bird informant.

Although the professional folklorist may delight in such details, he will not, unfortunately, consider them adequate justification for publication by his scholarly society. There are, however, two very good reasons why professional folklorists should read *Tales from the Basotho*. One is the fact that it is, of course, a translation. The other is that the tales of a Black South African race are presented to White South Africa by one of their own group in the knowledge that a faithful production of those tales will win admiration for their virtuosity and respect for the tribal performers of the tales.

For the first point, I refer to the trichotomy, belonging I suppose to Alan Dundes, of text, context, and texture. Briefly the *text* is what the story says on the surface, the narrative line. The *context* is the situation of the tale performance, a situation that gives to a performance its particular meaning: what kind of a teller performed for what kind of an audience when and where under what social, economic, or political conditions. The *texture* is the stylistic formularization that makes the tale seem like a folktale instead of a popular or literary short story. The text is easily determined. The context can be determined by anyone who has been trained to look for it and to appreciate its significance. The texture can be sensed by anyone who is completely at home with the language in which the tale has been performed and who is in full sympathetic understanding of the folk for whom the tale is performed. Even this paragon of sympathy and knowledge may have trouble defining, except perhaps by example, that texture. And while it is quite possible to give a good idea of text in a translation, and it is even probable that translation can give a good understanding of context, it is usually felt that texture is impossible to translate. It's easy to point out "Once upon a time" and "they lived happily ever after" as parts of the texture of English tales, but what is the distinguish-

ing texture of a Malay tale or a Chippewa fable? And why do trans-
lations of Zuñi myth sound either like gibberish or like stray seg-
ments of the King James Bible?

This is not the place to debate those questions, but the point is
that *Tales from the Basotho* is a translation, indeed a kind of lin-
guistic double play from Sesotho to Afrikaans to English. Yet I
think most readers will feel instantly that these are folktales. And
they will not feel so because these tales have a shadowy resemblance
to the style of English folktales. I don't know Afrikaans, but I would
suppose that these tales also don't resemble in style Afrikaans folktales. Certainly, I don't know Sesotho, and so I can't make any ridic-
ulous claims for their similarity in style to Sesotho tales. Perhaps no
one can give the exact effect of folkstyle in a quite different language. How could it be measured or determined except perhaps by
someone absolutely bilingual in the two languages in question? Be
that as it may, these Basotho tales somehow convey the impression
of alien folktales expertly and coherently performed. Perhaps judi-
cious use of simple, understandable, but uncustomary formulas and
of a rather peculiar repetition is one key to the creation of this sense
of texture. Whatever the secret, both Minnie Postma, who has done
it in Afrikaans, and Susie McDermid, who has done it in English,
deserve high praise.

The other point is a more ticklish one in these days of extraor-
dinary sensitivity in matters ethnic or racial. I am going to say it
right out in public, knowing it may not be understood as the
high praise I intend it to be: in many ways Minnie Postma must
be the Joel Chandler Harris of South Africa. Whatever his reasons,
Joel Chandler Harris did attempt to put on paper folktales that he
considered gems of narrative beauty and proverbial wisdom and
that his peers had ignored as the paltry mouthings of an enslaved
people who could be considered as, at best, simple irresponsible
children incapable of, and unworthy of, the good things in life. And
in his effort to give texture to his tales, Harris created for them on

paper a representation of a dialect that was variously considered
scarcely intelligible, laughably ignorant, scandalously inaccurate,
and most certainly not a vehicle for an art form. Harris turned the
black (as he thought them to be) folktales of Uncle Remus into the
standard entertainment for many generations of white children,
wherever the dialect could be read. That much has to be granted
Harris, whatever harm he unintentionally did by creating stereo-
types of Negro subservience, happy-go-luckiness, and role-accept-
ance.

So far as one can tell from this volume, Mrs. Postma has wisely
done nothing to create a stereotype Mosotho, favorable or unfavor-
able, to match Harris' Uncle Remus and Daddy Jake, but she has
given the impression of a justly proud Basotho folktale trove and
narrative performance of that trove that comes through into a foreign language as few other folktale collections have.

Wm. Hugh Jansen, the Editor

TRANSLATOR'S INTRODUCTION

In the mountainous country of Lesotho, landlocked inside the Republic of South Africa, the Basotho people still live a simple rural life. The winds of change, blowing down Africa, brought independence from Britain to this little country of only 11,716 mountainous square miles and less than a million people in 1966. In Maseru, the small-town capital, the music of the Beatles is heard these days, there are plastic gadgets in the one or two trading stores, and the men have exchanged their brightly colored woolen blankets (made in Manchester) for western suits. But a few miles away, in the mud-hut villages scattered through the high mountain valleys, life continues much as it has since Moshweshwe, their first king, gathered together the wandering tribes of the region and founded the Basotho nation early in the nineteenth century.

Today many of the men leave their homes to work in the gold mines of the Republic of South Africa, but the women and children and old folk remain in the villages, planting the crops and tending the cattle that supply most of their needs. Their huts are built of clay and thatched with reeds, and a reed screen in front of the huts supplies privacy and shelter. Behind the screens the little dung fires burn smokily at night, for the mountains of Lesotho are bare and devoid of trees, and firewood is a scarce commodity.

Later in the evening, when the food has been cooked and eaten, the children wheedle the older ones for stories. A single taboo about folk stories is in operation: no one must tell a story while the sun is shining, for then horns will grow from his head. This taboo, which is observed less and less in modern days, probably functioned to avoid wasting daylight hours with storytelling.

The stories serve no particular purpose other than one of entertainment. They do not even seem to point out morals, and in some stories virtue seems to be of no consequence and has no reward, as in the story of Mothemelle, the big bird, in which the unkind and unfeeling sister receives a reward equal to that of the kind and sympathetic one. The stories simply serve to while away the evening hours, for there is no electricity and no lamplight, and reading is still largely an unknown pastime. However, Lesotho has one of the highest percentages of school attendance of all Africa, and these evening story sessions might soon be no more than a memory.

In E. Jacottet's *Folk Tales of the Basuto*, Calloway writes that

[they are] children's tales now, but not the invention of a child's intellect, nor all invented to gratify a child's fancy. The stories which are transmitted orally from one generation to another deserve to arrest the attention of the anthropologist, the historian and the philosopher. They take us back, as it were, to the earlier ages of humanity, show us what were the conditions and environment in which our forefathers lived, and more faithfully perhaps than anything else, give us an insight into the working of the primitive human mind. If anything can be considered now as beyond any possible doubt, it is the antiquity of the folk tales. They are, in their general tenor and sometimes even in many of their details, older than the oldest literary monuments of the ancient world.

Nothing enables us better than the study of folklore to see that the human is practically the same under all climes, and among all races of mankind, civilised or still barbarian.

All the black nations of Africa south of the Sahara have their origins in the lake districts of Central Africa. There is no similarity

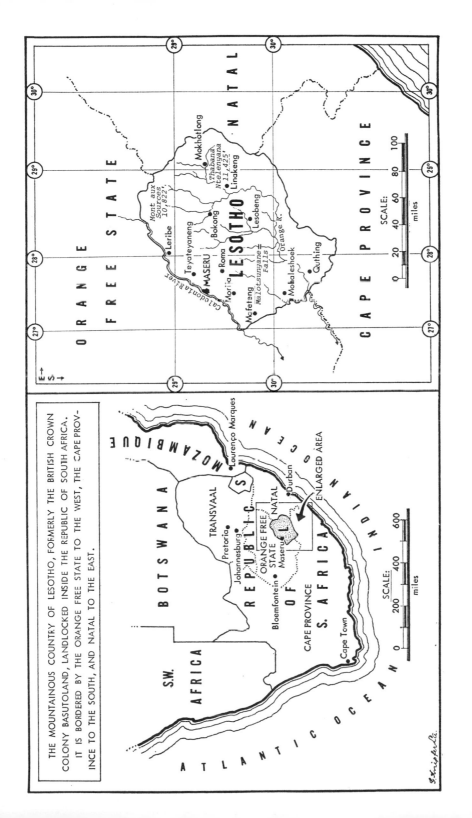

THE MOUNTAINOUS COUNTRY OF LESOTHO, FORMERLY THE BRITISH CROWN COLONY BASUTOLAND, LANDLOCKED INSIDE THE REPUBLIC OF SOUTH AFRICA. IT IS BORDERED BY THE ORANGE FREE STATE TO THE WEST, THE CAPE PROVINCE TO THE SOUTH, AND NATAL TO THE EAST.

ORANGE FREE STATE

NATAL

CAPE PROVINCE

Mokhotlong
Thabana Ntelenyana 11,425'
Linakeng
Mont aux Sources 10,822'
Leribe
Teyateyaneng
Bokong
Lesobeng
MASERU
Roma
Moria
LESOTHO
Orange R.
Maletsunyane Falls
Mafeteng
Mohaleshoek
Quthing
Caledon River

SCALE:
0   20   40   60   80   100
miles

E →
S →

MOZAMBIQUE

Lourenço Marques

S.W. AFRICA

BOTSWANA

TRANSVAAL

Pretoria
Johannesburg

REPUBLIC

OF

S. AFRICA

ORANGE FREE STATE

NATAL

Durban

Bloemfontein

Maseru

CAPE PROVINCE

Cape Town

ATLANTIC OCEAN

INDIAN OCEAN

ENLARGED AREA

SCALE:
0   200   400   600
miles

of language left, but the myths and legends of the many races are amazingly alike. Names differ, as may incidents in the stories, but the basic structure and the plots remain the same. During the centuries, the stories have acquired variations according to the history of the tribes concerned. The story of Tselane is a good example of this. In the original version of the story she was a black girl, but in later versions of the story she is a white girl with long hair, who lived in a strange white hut with wheels, with oxen drawing such huts by their tails. This represents, of course, the Dutch Voortrekker pioneers of a century and a half ago, who traveled northward much the same way as the American pioneers traveled westward in their covered wagons.

The audience may or may not join in when a song is part of the stories, but otherwise it does not participate. The storytelling of the Basotho is quite an art, and the simplest story becomes a thing of beauty when handled by a competent raconteur. He or she speaks in a soft, musical voice and uses many facial expressions and gesticulations as embellishments. Great care is taken to maintain a perfect sense of rhythm, and, if the storyteller feels that something is amiss with the rhythm, he will repeat a word or part of a word, a phrase, sometimes a whole sentence until the rhythm is to his satisfaction. Even whole paragraphs are repeated, to the increased joy of the listeners.

The Basotho storyteller wastes no time with an introduction of the "once upon a time there was a chief who had three daughters . . ." type. He simply begins his story with "They say that the eldest of the chief's daughters . . ." or "They tell of the time the daughter of the chief." . . . Nor does the storyteller work his story up to a climax or use any suspense. Since the audience probably knows the outcome of the story anyway, the attraction lies not in the content but in the manner in which the story is told.

Many white people may speak the Sesotho language quite fluently, especially those who live in the Orange Free State, near Lesotho, and come into contact with the people of Lesotho. But no matter how fluently the white man may speak the language, he is in most cases still unable to reach the Basotho world of thought and feeling (Lesotho is the country; Sesotho the language; Mosotho is a denizen of the country; Basotho is both the collective or plural people and the adjective relating to the country and its people). Therefore, to many white people it is a revelation to discover that the Basotho have a rich heritage of myths and legends perhaps thousands of years old with origins in countries as remote as India or ancient Greece at the dawn of civilization. It is also a surprise to discover tales of the Western world in Basotho dress, such as that of Seendire-la (Cinderella) who met the brave young chief, resplendent in his leopard skin robe, at the tribal gathering.

Minnie Postma is one of the white people who have complete understanding and sympathy with the Basotho's thoughts and feelings. She spent her childhood on a farm bordering Lesotho, learning Sesotho from babyhood together with her own Afrikaans, the language of Dutch derivation spoken in South Africa. The children of the Basotho workers on her parents' farm were the playmates of Minnie Postma, and soon she knew the stories of the Basotho people better than she did those of Red Riding Hood or Snow White. Not only were her parents fluent enough in Sesotho to tell her many of the legends, but every evening, when the supper dishes had been washed and put away, it was also "*tsomo* time" in the kitchen. The white children and the Basotho house servants would sit together on the kitchen floor by the warmth of the wood stove, and the myths and legends of the Basotho would be told over and over again. It was a ritual that the storyteller would be, or pretend to be, reluctant to tell a story and had to be cajoled and teased into acquiescence, more often than not being bribed with a length of chewing tobacco or a few pieces of candy. Then the story would unfold by the light of a

flickering candle, while handfuls of dried corn cobs would be tossed
into the fire from time to time to keep the embers alive and com-
fortingly warm.

Since girlhood Minnie Postma has made notes of these stories in
their many variations. No two storytellers would ever tell the same
version of a story. One raconteur would not even tell the story the
same way twice in succession, for the mood of the teller and the
reaction of the audience would often determine the variations that
would go into the telling.

She also made notes of the stories that she wheedled out of the
elderly Basotho folk she met. The old ones are almost the only ones
left who are familiar with the *litsomo*, for the youth in Lesotho are
like youth the world over, far more interested in pop music and
the entertainment heroes of the day than in the rich heritage of their
own folklore.

In South Africa most white children of middle class have black
"nannies," whose principal function seems to be to keep their small
white charges out of mischief and out of their parents' hair. While
the white mother may tend to the child's important needs, such as
feeding, putting to bed, and bathing, the nanny is the one who baby-
sits and entertains. Much of the entertainment is the telling of
stories, and as result the white children of South Africa are far
more familiar with the folklore of their black neighbor races than,
say, the white American child is familiar with the folklore of American Indian tribes.

Often Minnie Postma would overhear nannies speaking Sesotho
among themselves in a park or on a beach; then she would speak
to them, asking them to tell her a story, in order to add it to her
collection.

She has avidly sought after and read any legends published in
English or Sesotho, including the collection of stories published by
the French missionaries of the Paris Evangelical Mission Society.

In time she became so familiar with the manner in which the

Basotho tell a story that she, too, could take a five-line jingle and embroider it into a *tsomo*, with the required length and all the poetic phraseology and repetitions and emphases that the Basotho use. Usually the tables were turned, and it was Mrs. Postma who told stories to Basotho audiences, who were amazed and amused that a white woman could make a "*tsomo* of the old people." When she married, her new in-laws were enchanted with the stories, and soon she found herself providing regular after-dinner entertainment whenever family and friends gathered.

About twenty years ago she began to write the stories, the major works being published in Afrikaans. They were *Legendes uit die Misrook* [Legends from the smoke of the dung fire], *Legendes uit Basoetoeland*, and *Litsomo*. Then there was *Bulane*, originally written for the radio but later rewritten as a book, and *Ons Maak die Kleipot oop* [We open the clay pot], now also a book after first appearing as a series of radio talks on the ways of life of the Basotho. She has also often told stories over the radio, singing the accompanying songs that illuminate the stories, and has presented this kind of entertainment at many a club meeting or dinner in South Africa.

Minnie Postma's quest after folklore is still not finished. Only recently, when teaching in the district of the Transvaal town Louis Trichardt, she heard and recorded some *tsomos* that she had never heard before.

The Basotho stories can roughly be classified into three categories: myths, animal stories, and domestic stories that do not contain any miraculous element at all. Sometimes the three overlap.

To the first category belongs the tender story of the origin of man. The first four people in the world were men, who were frightened and alarmed when they became aware of a strange creature living on an adjoining hill. At first they descended on her like birds of prey, only to discover that she was gentle like a fawn and needed their protection and hunting skills. In return she showed them how to cook food and made warm clothes from the skins of the animals they killed.

Many of the stories are cruel and bloodthirsty in the extreme; others are crude and even vulgar, a relic of a time when the Basotho lived a primitive and harsh life, when such processes as elimination and sex took place with little privacy or inhibition.

Many myths exist about the childless woman, the *nyopa*, for in this primitive society childlessness is a tragedy. The schemes that the witch doctors devise to help these outcast *linyopa* make many a fascinating tale. The witch doctor not only helps the childless woman to bear children, but he also restores health to the sick and brings rain to the drought-stricken areas. If he is paid enough he will help people to be avenged for the wrongs done by their enemies —perhaps by sending a snake to eat their intestines from within.

The heroes and heroines of the myths and the domestic stories are always the chiefs and their wives, their sons and their daughters. The names do not matter much. The brave and handsome young warrior is almost always Masilo or Bulane, and the maiden is Tselane or Thakáne. There may be other names, but, if the storyteller momentarily forgets the name, he will have no qualms about substituting one of the other favorite names on the spur of the moment.

The maidens are usually so beautiful that they shine with a special light of their own. Even the light of the sun dims when such a maiden emerges from her hut. Plumpness is beautiful, for it brings a much admired yellow color to the face; in contrast, one who is starving and undernourished will become "black from thinness."

There are a myriad of stories about love in its many forms— the love between man and animal, parent and child, brother and sister as well as the love between a man and a woman, with or without the bonds of marriage. Thus arise the stories that deal with the unhappiness caused by polygamy, also jealously and envy and hatred and bitterness between the children, especially when a half-brother and a half-sister fall in love, unaware of their kinship. The Basotho regard such a love as unnatural and evil.

In many a story there is an old woman of the village—crafty and wise and with many privileges. The young woman who goes off into the world will encounter the old one along the way, bewailing her dreadful diseases. She pleads pitifully that the young one should stay and help her. If she continues on her way without stopping, she will also go without the sage advice of the old one. If she stays to help and comfort, she receives detailed advice on coping with the obstacles awaiting her and eventually marries the handsome son of the chief, who gives her many skin blankets, many pots, many beads, and many children.

Some stories tell of how the old one is killed by a wicked man or woman and cooked while everyone is away tilling the fields. The cruel death is only discovered when someone finds a toe or a finger in the stewpot.

Revenge is a popular theme. A vengeful man or woman is seldom satisfied with anything less than death. This death comes in many forms: the food may be poisoned; the victim may be pushed into a crevasse in the mountains; the revenger may wait until the victim crawls into the cave where clay is gathered and then dance on the roof so that the roof falls in and smothers the victim; or a witch doctor may be paid to change him into an ant heap or "bury" him in the stomach of a cannibal.

That the fear of cannibalism was widespread in bygone days is obvious from the many legends about the *limo*, or *lelimo*. Apart from the ordinary cannibalistic *limo*, there are many other monsters: Kholumolumo, big as a mountain, who ate a whole tribe, including chickens and beasts of burden; the white Heletuma who ate a whole wedding party, "bride price" cattle and all; Obe, who sings a whole village to sleep with his sweet voice and carries off the young women one by one in his immense ears, to eat them later;

Nanabolele, with a skin that shines in the dark, who sleeps off his cannibalistic orgies in his home beneath the deep waters of the permanent pools that are fed by the flash floods of the mountains.

A popular figure is Moselantja, or Pulmagazan, a heartless woman with a hideous tail ending in a mouth with an insatiable appetite. During the day she hides the tail under her skirts, but at night the tail emerges to hunt for its favorite food, milk. The greed of the tail is the end of Moselantja. After she is put to death, she arises again in the form of a pumpkin plant that causes more misery. When the people of the village stab the pumpkin with spears, blood flows from the wounds. Still Pulmagazan is not dead, for then she lives in the form of insects and lice in the thatched roof of the hut of her enemy and comes out at night to attack. The hut is set on fire—but Pulmagazan lives on, this time as thorns in the path where the children of the hated one walk.

The romantic figure is Monyohe, the great snake of the deep pools, who casts a covetous eye on the daughter of the chief as she comes to dip water. Sometimes he beats her with his tail, as any right-minded Mosotho will beat his wife with a stick. In one story, remarkably reminiscent of the Greek myth of Eros and Psyche, he is the mysterious and invisible bridegroom-beast who comes to visit his bride at dead of night, when he cannot be seen. Invariably he is restored to human form: a brave young man, strong as a bull, an iron blanket over his shoulders, and his stick is no less than the horn of the mighty rhinoceros!

The hero of the animal stories is clever Rabbit, who outwits even the Lion. Naturally Rabbit is always in trouble, but he is the one who can run away the fastest, and he will even disguise himself by cutting off his ears and sitting right in the middle of the road with the raggedy ear-stumps, confident that no one will recognize him.

A rustic peace and beauty pervade the stories, which Minnie Postma has taken care to bring into her version of the tales. The feared Koeoko will, for instance, be pulling the only son of the chief underneath the waters: at the same time, the mother, unaware of the danger, is hoeing the fields with the other women; the boys are trapping little birds in the hills; the girls, each with a baby tied to her back, are digging for edible bulbs in the veld; the old women will be dreaming in the gentle sunlight in front of the huts; and the old men, too old for man's work, will be hunting for firewood.

Minnie Postma has told the stories in the same style as the Basotho do; with all the exclamations and repetitions that are normally used; and she gives many a glimpse into the tribal life that is already a thing of the past in some areas, although still existing in others, where skin blankets are still worn and the young boys and girls still go to their separate "schools of initiation" before emerging as men and women of the tribe.

TALES FROM THE BASOTHO

1. The Giant Bird Mothemelle

Many years ago a giant bird flew around the Luti Mountains in Basutoland. He lived there. His name was Mothemelle. When he called, the canyons answered. And when he flew up in the sky the sun grew dark, so big was he, that Mothemelle. He could lift a person from the ground and fly away with him, as a hawk flies away with a little chicken. *Yo,* when that bird cried up there in the sky all the children ran to hide under the blankets their mothers wore, until he went away again. But he was not a bad bird. His heart was white. No, his heart was white.

Now the old people tell of the two daughters of the chief Bulane. There was the big daughter and the one who was younger than she. They were very beautiful, those girls, but the first one was more beautiful than her sister.

They lived in the days before people ate sorghum, the kafir corn. They did not eat sorghum, for it was food for the cattle. But the big daughter of Bulane wanted to grind some of the kernels and cook them so that she could see what sorghum tasted like. But her mother would not allow it. Her father would not allow it either.

But her head was hard. One day she waited until they had gone to work in the fields, and then she took some kafir corn, and she ground it in the hollowed stump that they used for grinding their usual corn, and when it was just right she half filled a big pot with the ground corn and put it on the fire to cook. And while she waited for it to cook, she went to the spring to fetch water. Her younger sister went with her.

But when they came back, the kafir corn filled the pot! It was a strange business. They could not understand it at all.

The big daughter scooped out a dish full of the kernels. They had swelled, and they were soft! She was amazed. She ate a handful and it tasted good. She gave some to her sister, and her sister also said it was good. They ate some more. After that they covered the pot again.

Then they swept the floor of the hut, and when they stopped to listen they heard *tlerre-e-eh, sho-aaaa*, as the lid fell off the pot.

"*Mè wheh!* Mother mine!" shouted the little one. "The corn has done this. See how full the pot is again! It is getting more and more! The corn is surely bewitched!"

Now the big girl became very scared, for the sorghum kept increasing in the pot. It covered the floor. The whole reed shelter was soon full of corn, and their fear for the anger of their parents increased as fast as the corn increased.

"You see," said the little one, "our parents said we must not cook this corn. But you did not listen. They will surely kill you, because it is you who brought this evil to their house."

"I will run away," said the big one. "They will not catch me."

Then she hung her blanket over her shoulders and fled to the mountains. She ran quickly. It was the middle of the day, but suddenly it was dark around her.

She looked up to see where the big cloud had come from so quickly, but she saw no cloud. It was the big bird. Mothemelle. It was he. It was he who flew in front of the sun with his big wings.

He will help me, she thought. And she called him with a song that echoed through the mountains:

Mothemelle-themelle,

Take me up above, Mothemelle-themelle,
Mother has said, Mothemelle-themelle,
Do not cook, Mothemelle-themelle,
Corn is food, Mothemelle-themelle,
For the herd of Bulane, Mothemelle-themelle.

The giant bird heard her. He came down, he came down. He scooped her up gently with one wing, and with the other he flew, over the mountains to a place where no man lived. Then he put her down on the ground and flew away.

Now she was altogether alone and afraid of the night that was coming. When it began to grow dark, she saw a little smoke curling in the sky from behind a clump of bushes. She walked through the bushes as light of foot as a partridge, to go and see whether there were people she could join.

She walked, she walked, she walked through the bushes. She came to the end of the bushes, and she peeped through the leaves and saw some young men sitting by the fire, cooking meat. She was too shy to speak to them and was just about to disappear again among the bushes when one of the young men saw her.

It was Masilo, the son of the chief. All his life he had been unable to speak, but, when he saw the beautiful young girl darting away, his voice was loosened and he shouted: "Men, see that beautiful girl! Catch her! Quickly! Before she disappears!"

They caught her and took her to their master. *Au*, he was very glad to see her. And he talked nicely to her so that her heart could lie down. And when he saw that her heart was lying quietly, he told his men to give her some meat to eat.

She ate, and then they all lay down to sleep beside the fire.

When the dark grew light, the men went to their huts, and Masilo took the girl to his father, he who was the supreme chief of his tribe, and he told the big man that he wanted to marry the girl.

The chief was satisfied, for it was a great miracle that the girl had brought to his dumb son. He gave his permission, and they held a great feast to celebrate the marriage.

And when they had two children she thought it would be safe to go back to her own people so that they could see her husband and her two beautiful fat children.

Chè, the chief said it was right so. Then he would send forty cows to the father of his daughter-in-law, to pay for the girl. And also a saddle horse and goats and sheep. That was what her father should get, because his daughter had married Masilo. That was as it should be.

Au mè, it was a beautiful visit, that one! The daughter put on her most beautiful clothes, she hung her new skin blanket round her shoulders, and her beads sparkled like the sun round her neck, her arms, her waist, her legs. No, it was a beautiful visit.

The chief Bulane received the forty cows together with the other animals and the saddle horse.

The wife of the chief received clay pots and sleeping mats. She received loads of dried dung, already prepared for smearing on the floors of their huts, and she received many calabashes and gourds and a blanket made from the skins of jackals, a long one that hung to her feet.

Their hearts were so happy about all the beautiful gifts and about the beautiful fat grandchildren that they never scolded about the kafir corn that their big daughter had cooked.

When they had finished visiting they went back to their own home, and the hearts of the old people were sore because their children lived so far away. They were sad, and that made their other daughter, the younger one, very jealous. The jealousy over her sister who was so happy began to boil in her like the kafir corn had boiled in the pot on the fire, and when it pushed open the lid of her heart the whole hut was filled with her jealousy.

Her parents could not bear it. They chased her away and she ran

to the mountains. It was still early in the day, but when she looked
around her it was dark. When she looked up in the sky she saw it
was the giant bird Mothemelle that had come between her and the
sun.

Then she made a plan. She would do exactly as her sister had
done, and then Mothemelle would also take her to that place where
her sister lived, and then she would also get such nice clothes and
such a rich husband and such beautiful fat children. She called
the bird:

Mothemelle-themelle,

Take me up above, Mothemelle-themelle,

Mother has said, Mothemelle-themelle,

Do not cook, Mothemelle-themelle,

Corn is food, Mothemelle-themelle,

For the herd of Bulane, Mothemelle-themelle.

But from the sky the giant bird replied: "You are lying to me.
It is not sorghum you have boiled. It is jealousy. You fight the whole
day long. You have filled the *lapa*, the court of your parents' home,
with disunity and dissatisfaction. You can flee from the corn, but
you cannot get away from that! You will take it with you wherever
you go, even under my wing up here in the sky."

But she kept begging:

Mothemelle-themelle,

Take me up above, Mothemelle-themelle,

Take me up above, Mothemelle-themelle.

And when she kept on begging like that, the big bird snatched
her. He snatched her and flew with her to a far land. She thought
this was where her sister lived with her rich husband and her beautiful fat children, but she did not see any people. She did not see the
people of the land, because it was the land of the maneaters, who
lived in villages under the ground, under the deep pools of water.
She did not know it, but they had already seen her. They saw where

the giant bird put her down, and their hearts were glad about the good meat that the bird had brought them. Their hearts were very glad.

When the girl sat down and wondered what she should do next, a woman came up to her. She leaned on a stick, for she was very old.

"Young girl," said she. "You must not sit here. You must flee."

"Go away!" replied the girl. "Who gave you the right to speak to me? Your mind has gone away from you! I am waiting for my sister."

"It is not here where your sister is. Beneath these waters the maneaters live. And they are already cleaning the pots to cook you tonight. Perhaps I do not still have the brains of a young girl, but even so I have more brains than you! And I tell you that you must flee at once. This is advice that you must follow."

Then the old woman walked away. She leaned on her stick. She walked to the side of the pool and then disappeared under the water. Then the girl knew that the old one belonged with the maneaters who lived under the water.

She became very frightened because it grew dark, and she was alone. She heard the big bird cry from afar, and she called to him:

Mothemelle-themelle,

Please come and fetch me, Mothemelle-themelle,

To my home, Mothemelle-themelle.

But he did not come to get her. He flew farther away, farther. He went to his nest in a gorge in the Luti Mountains.

She kept on calling, but he did not come. Then she began to run. She ran along the river to find a shallow place where she could cross. But the stream became broader. It became deeper. She turned round and ran back, because the river was narrower higher up. She ran right to its source, but there the water had cut such a deep channel into the mountainside that still she could not cross it. And the more she struggled to find a place to cross, the more annoyed she became with Mothemelle. Eventually she came to a place where a tree trunk formed a bridge across the stream. There she crossed it, for on the other side was the region where her father lived.

"When I get home I'll get my people to kill that bird, for it is he who has landed me in this trouble," she said. Then she began to walk home.

She walked. She came to a spring. At the spring was a crippled woman who was struggling to put a clay pot full of water on her head.

"Please help me, young girl," pleaded the woman. "I cannot lift the water on to my head."

But the sulky girl said: "Can't you see I am so tired I could die, Woman-with-the-clay-pot? Rather give me some water to drink. Hurry up! The thirst is choking me."

The woman dipped a calabash of water from the clay pot and gave it to the girl. But she would not drink it. She sloshed it out of the calabash.

"What sort of a person are you?" she asked of Woman-with-the-clay-pot. "Your dipping calabash is stinking. Do you want the daughter of Chief Bulane to drink from such a stinking thing? If you want that calabash again, you can go and pick it up yourself." And she threw the calabash into the bushes.

Then she walked on. She walked until she came to a village of mud huts. She went inside one of the houses and there she found a woman kneeling as she ground corn.

"What kind of a person are you?" she asked Woman-with-the-grindstone. "Your dirty blouse is hanging in the corn you are grinding!"

"Are you talking to me, *nake*, beloved?" asked Woman-with-the-grindstone.

"I am not your beloved," said the girl. "What sort of a person are you to call a stranger *nake*?"

She went away from there also and walked until she came to the hut of an old woman.

"I am hungry and thirsty, old woman. Give me food."

"There is corn in the pot on the fire, young girl. Take enough to satisfy you," she said. "The people of my house can eat what remains in the pot after you have done."

But the girl threw all the corn out of the pot on to the blanket of the old woman, and after the water had drained off she gathered up the blanket by its corners and tied it round her body. And she walked on.

She walked for two days, and then she came to the village where the brother of her mother lived. They were glad to see her and told her they would find a husband for her if she would stay with them.

She said no, it was good so. Then her uncle found a husband for her. He found one that would take out enough cattle for her, enough cattle out of his herd to pay the bride price, but she said: "H-h-ha! Such an ugly thing! Worm! I do not want to see him. My sister has a husband much handsomer than he."

Then they found another man for her, but she said: "H-h-ha! Such an old creature! My sister's husband is young. Who said I wanted a baboon for a husband?"

After the old man the uncle found another husband for her, and another, and many others, but she was satisfied with no one. "You make me tired, girl," said her uncle. "You are a person that we cannot satisfy. You make out that all the men in this place are bad. All the hearts are upset. There is only one plan: you must go away. Go!"

Yo, yo, it was a bad thing! She could not wait. She ran out through the door and took the road to the village of her father. And as she ran she called to Mothemelle to come and fetch her:

Please come and get me, Mothemelle-themelle,
Please come and get me, Mothemelle-themelle,
Please come and get me, Mothemelle-themelle.

But he did not come at all. Then she walked farther. She walked the whole day, and then she slept. She walked another day, and then she slept again. She walked many days until she came to the place where her parents lived.

Her mother and her father were very glad to have their child back again. They gave her beautiful clothes to wear, they gave her much food to eat, they let her rest in comfort, and, when she was fully rested, the chief said there was a young man who had come to speak to him. He wanted her as wife.

"I first want to see what he looks like," she said. And when she saw him, she was satisfied.

"Will he also take out forty head of cattle from his herd, as the husband of my sister did for her?" she asked.

"He will," said her father.

"Will he also give me beautiful clothes and such ornaments, as my sister's husband gave to her?"

"Yes, he will."

"Will he give me a blanket made of the skins of jackals, as my sister's husband gave to her?"

"Yes, he will."

"Then it is good," she said. "But first Mothemelle must be killed. As long as that bird lives my heart will not lie down."

The chief wanted to satisfy his child, and he wanted to see his grandchildren before he died. So he sent a number of his brave hunters to kill Mothemelle. And after the giant bird was dead, his daughter was wed to the young man.

And this is the end of the story.

2. Wolf and Jackal and the Beautiful Girl

The old people tell of a girl. She was very beautiful. Wolf saw her, and he fell in love with her and wanted to marry her, because she was so beautiful. He talked about his beautiful betrothed all day long. He told Jackal how beautiful she was. He said that he was going to work very hard so that he could earn enough cattle to give to her father, enough cattle to pay the bride price for this beautiful girl. So he talked every day. Every day. *Yoalo. Yoalo.*

Yo, thought Jackal, that must indeed be a beautiful girl! He wanted Wolf to take him to the beautiful girl so that he could see for himself. But Wolf was too jealous of this girl that he was courting. Also, he did not trust Jackal. Not at all. For was not Jackal the wiliest of all the animals of the veld?

But Jackal made one of his clever plans. One day when Wolf went to court his girl, Jackal followed at a distance, and so he found out where the beautiful girl lived.

He waited until Wolf had finished courting for that day, and, when Wolf had left, Jackal went to the girl's house. *Au*, it was true what Wolf had said! She was beautiful! She shone more than the sun shone. He fell in love with her at once. His heart was very happy, and he talked with her and with her family. They sat and listened as he talked. They listened as he told stories to them. Some stories were sad, and then they all wept and their hearts were sore. Some stories were happy and funny, and then they all laughed and laughed. They laughed until they lay flat on the ground from so much laughing.

Yo, they liked this fellow who could tell so many stories!

Then he spoke to the girl, and he said: "My sister, I have heard many things about you."

"What did you hear, *Morena*?"

"I heard that you were a very beautiful girl."

She became shy and threw her *karos*, her skin blanket, over her face. Then she asked softly: "Who said that to you, *ná*?"

"It is my riding horse that said that to me. He never stops talking about you."

"Your riding horse?"

"Yes," he said. "My riding horse is a man who says he is betrothed to you."

"It is a lie," she replied. "I am not betrothed to a horse! What is his name?"

"His name? It is Wolf, my friend."

"*Chè*, Wolf is the name of the man to whom I am betrothed. But he is not the riding horse of any man."

"You will yet see it, Mother, then you will believe it."

The next time Wolf came a-courting his girl, everybody was very unfriendly toward him. Not only the girl was unfriendly, but her parents were unfriendly also. Her brothers and sisters also.

"Why is everybody unfriendly toward me today?" he asked the girl. She did not even look at him. She looked away as she said, "Because you are the riding horse of Jackal."

"Who says so?"

"He himself told us. That man Jackal told us."

Wolf was very annoyed about this. He said he was going to fetch Jackal immediately so that they could talk about the matter in front

of her parents. He took his walking stick and left. He walked straight
to the house of Jackal.

He was still a great distance away when Jackal saw him coming.
And then he knew at once that there was going to be trouble if he
did not think of a plan.

He began groaning loudly, and then he went to his mother. "*Mè*,"
he said, "please unroll my sleeping mat for me. I want to lie down.
The pains are biting inside me. I am very sick, Mother!"

The woman believed him. She believed him, and unrolled the mat
for him. He went to lie down, and he groaned and moaned so loudly
that she thought he was dying.

When Wolf arrived at that house, he heard Jackal groaning and
moaning. The big woman told him of the illness of her son. But
Wolf's heart was very hard. He said he did not care. Jackal had to
get up and come with him so that he could clear up the matter of the
riding horse with the beautiful girl and her people. Jackal had to
clear up the matter before he died.

Jackal pleaded with Wolf to leave him alone, because he was so
very ill, but Wolf said no, he must come.

Jackal said he was too weak to walk, Wolf must carry him. Wolf
said no, it was all right. He would carry Jackal. He was strong
enough, and he would carry the sick man on his back, and then at
the same time the beautiful girl would see how much strength there
was in the body of Wolf.

Jackal climbed on the back of Wolf. But as soon as he was up, he
fell off again.

"I can't help it, my good friend," said Jackal. "I am too weak to
sit by myself. I shall have to have a saddle."

So they put a saddle on Wolf's back, and Jackal climbed up
again. But as soon as he was up, he fell off again.

"I can't help it, my good friend," said Jackal. "I can't stay in the
saddle unless I have reins to hold on to. You will have to have a
bridle."

So Jackal's family put a bridle on Wolf and put the reins in Jackal's hands.

But he fell off again.

"I can't help it, Wolf. I can't stay in the saddle unless I have stirrups in which to rest my feet."

And then they gave him stirrups. And then he had to have shoes on his feet.

"Can't I please stay home?" Jackal pleaded.

"No," said Wolf. "You must come, so that you can confess your lies to my girl and her people."

"Then you must bring me my fur cap and my new skin blanket. See how I am shivering with cold," said Jackal. "The cold will make me more ill." And he groaned and moaned so loudly that Wolf was afraid that he would die before they even set out for the home of the girl and her family. And they gave him his new fur cap and his new skin blanket.

"Now you will have to bring me two thorns so that I can pin the blanket round my neck and also round my stomach, or the wind will whip it from my body," said Jackal.

They did so. But still Jackal was not satisfied.

"The flies are bothering me," said he. "Look how they are swarming over me! Bring me a bunch of twigs so that I can chase them away."

They brought him a bunch of twigs, and, when Jackal had everything that he had asked for, he pleaded: "Can't I please stay home in bed?"

But Wolf said no. They must go at once. But Jackal was moaning and groaning so terribly! More and more! Louder and louder!

When Wolf and Jackal came near the hut where the girl lived, the dogs started to bark and the people knew that the dogs had seen or heard something.

The girl made an opening in the reed screen in front of the hut and looked through it to see why the dogs were barking so. Jackal saw her peering through the opening, and immediately he sat up straight. He sat up straight like a chief of the tribe. He pulled out the thorn that held the skin blanket across his stomach and gripped it between his toes. And he used it as a spur to prick Wolf in the stomach, so that he should run faster and faster. Just as a real horse carries a rich man!

Jackal, the rich man with his fur cap and his new skin blanket!

He stopped in front of the *lapa*, the talking place of the girl's home, and quickly jumped from Wolf's back. He gave Wolf a smart whack with the twigs that he carried in his hand, but Wolf was so tired that he did not even jump. He was quite out of breath. On his head was a bridle, on his back was a saddle, and at his sides hung stirrups for the feet of the rider.

"Now do you see, Big Woman?" Jackal asked of the beautiful girl. "Did I speak the truth or did I tell a lie when I said that you had betrothed yourself to my riding horse?"

"No, you spoke the truth, Father," said she. "I thank you for warning me before it was too late."

Wolf fell down to the ground when they unsaddled him. So tired was he.

Jackal and the girl drank a whole clay pot of beer with her people. And then he became the betrothed of the girl, and here the story comes to an end.

3. The Outcast

The old people tell the tale of a girl who was rejected by her people. The name of the girl was Molisa-oa-Lipoli— the tender of the goats. She tended the goats.

She had to work very hard. It was she who had to grind the corn, and it was she who had to cook the corn porridge for the whole household. But she herself did not dare to eat any of it. When she wanted to eat the crumbs that clung to the stick after she had finished stirring the porridge, they snatched the stick out of her hands and beat her over the head with it. She was black from hunger and thinness, for she had to work all day with a stomach that was cold. And at night she had to go to sleep with a stomach that was cold.

But the heart of the mother of her mother was very soft. She felt sorry for Molisa. She comforted her when the others beat her, and every day, when the girl went to the veld with the goats, the old one secretly brought her some food.

One day when Molisa again ate the crumbs from the porridge stick, her mother grabbed it out of her hands and hit her over the head with it. She hit Molisa-oa-Lipoli. Then they all threw stones and rocks at her and chased her away. She ran, they threw. She ran until they could not see her any more.

She did not come back again. She ran until she was so tired that she could not go any farther. So she sat down on the ground to rest a while.

The spirits of her forefathers saw her, and presently a hand that she could not see put down some food on the ground. But even though Molisa was very hungry, she did not eat it. She was afraid that the food might be bewitched and had been put down there by her people in order to poison her. No, she did not eat it. She got up and ran away from that food that was so strange to her.

She walked the whole day, she walked, and every time she sat down to rest she saw that the bowl of food was again on the ground beside her.

When it was evening she was so hungry that she dared to eat the food.

She ate it. She ate it all. She finished it. And it did not kill her at all.

She lay down on the ground and went to sleep. And when she woke up, she was still alive. She was still alive, and beside her stood the bowl of food.

She ate it. She ate it.

Molisa-oa-Lipoli walked farther, and always the spirits of her forefathers looked after her. Many days went by, and she kept on walking until she came to a mountain. On the slopes of the mountain she saw a nice hut. A new, nice hut, with a big, round screen of reeds in front of it.

One heart of Molisa was glad, but the other heart was afraid of the unknown. She went nearer, slowly, slowly, slowly. But when she peeped round the screen, she saw no strange woman inside. She hesitantly looked inside the hut, but there was no one there either.

She wondered, she wondered. And she went outside to sit down on the little mud wall beside the door. She waited. Maybe the owners of this quiet hut had gone to the fields. Maybe they had gone out to gather cow dung. She did not know.

But just as she was about to sit down, she saw the bowl of food there again. And water in a clay pot.

She washed her hands. Then she ate.

By evening the same hands that had brought her the food made a fire inside the shelter. She went to sit beside the fire. She sat until it was dark. Then she lay down where she had been sitting, and she went to sleep.

But when the dark became light again, she woke up and saw that she was lying inside the hut, and not beside the fire. She lay on a sleeping mat. And over her body skin blankets had been spread. Next to her were clothes that would fit her. Beads also. Rings also. Rings for her arms and rings for her legs. At first she did not want to put the clothes on, but when she looked for her own rags, she saw that they were smoldering on the fire.

Chè! Now she could not help but put on the strange clothes. She did so. They were very nice clothes. Like the clothes of the wife of a chief.

From then on she lived like the wife of a *morena*, a chief. She did no work at all. She did not even sweep out the hut and the shelter behind the screen—everything was done for her. She lived a good life, but the loneliness was hard to bear. But when she woke up one morning, she was no longer alone. The hands who looked after her had brought a child to her. Her joy was great, because it was a boy child. But her heart was not yet altogether happy, for there was no one she could show that boy child to.

She wished her old grandmother could see the baby, and then she decided to go and show the baby to the old one.

When she came to her own people they were amazed to see that the outcast wore such nice clothes and had such a beautiful boy child in the *thari* on her back. She walked just like the wife of a chief! She leaned on a stick, and over her head she held a shelter against the sun. Oh, she shone! But she pretended that she did not

know them, and she greeted only the mother of her mother. And
when the old woman had seen the child, Molisa wanted to go back
to her hut. But first she asked the old woman to give her someone to
help her look after the child.

Chè, it is right so. The old one chose one of her many granddaugh-
ters to go back with Molisa.

And now that the young mother had someone to help her take
care of the child, her heart longed for a little field that she could till,
where she could grow pumpkins and corn, watermelons and sweet
reeds for herself and the child. She knew just where the field should
be, against the side of the mountain, on the other side of the creek.
But she did not have an iron pick with which to break the ground,
and she did not have any seeds either.

She went to sleep, and when she woke up she saw an iron pick
waiting for her. And seeds also. *Yo*—she was glad!

Every day, every day, she tilled her little field. But one day her
seeds were done. She took the child and sent the young girl to her
home to fetch more seeds.

When the girl returned, she saw a thing she could not understand.
Beside their hut stood many huts. And people were living in them:
men, women, and children. There were ash heaps outside the village
and chickens scratching in the ground beside the huts. There were
corrals made of branches, full of cattle.

The girl had such a fright that she ran away to fetch Molisa-oa-
Lipoli. The woman came to see what was going on, and, when she
saw the people, the huts, the corrals, and the ash heaps, she fainted.

When she opened her eyes again, she saw a handsome young man
sitting near her. He sat on the ground inside the shelter of the reed
screen in front of the hut. By his clothes she could see that he was a
chief.

He asked, "Where is your husband?"

She answered: "I haven't seen him yet, *Morena*. Only the child I
have seen."

Then he told her that he was her husband and that the child was his child. She believed him, because the child looked exactly like him. The little one immediately loved the man, even though it was the first time that he saw him.

Then they all lived together in the same house. The chief and his wife and their son lived in the same house, and in the many houses around them lived all their subjects. But the chief and his wife had two hearts. The one heart was happy, but the other heart had a worry: Molisa's people had not been punished. The people who had rejected Molisa and ill-treated her had not yet been punished.

But the hands that had tended her had not forgotten her. The spirits of her forefathers talked to the chief, and then he knew what he had to do.

First he gathered together much corn, much wheat, and much sorghum. He stored it all in great holes in the ground. And, when he had enough stored, the sun stood still. There was a drought, and a great famine came to the people of his wife. When they began to die of hunger, he sent some of his people to bite those people on the ears with the story that Molisa had much wheat, much sorghum. They could come and barter it for cattle.

Chè, it was good news! They brought their leather bags, they brought their grass baskets with lids. The grandmother sent her bag also.

It was like this. When the people arrived, they were black with hunger. Just as Molisa used to be. The chief gave them food to eat. And, while they ate, he told his men to fill the bags of Molisa's people.

They did so. They filled the bags. But only in the bag of the grandmother did they put food. In the bags of all the other people they put fine dung.

But the people did not know this. Only when they reached their own village did they see that there was no food in the bags, but dung that they could not eat.

It was an ugly business! "We must leave this place again," they said. "We must leave, and this time go over the mountains to the place where there is always food."

That night they all left. All left, except that grandmother of Molisa. And after a few days Molisa sent messengers to go and fetch the grandmother. She came to live with them. Molisa built a new hut for her near her own hut and took care of her until she died.

And that is the end of the story.

4. Fenya-fenyane

The old ones tell the story of Fenya-fenyane. She was the daughter of a great chief. She was so beautiful that the sun paled next to her. That was why she had the name of Fenya-fenyane: the one who excelled, the one who shone, the one who won. That was why.

Fenya-fenyane was to be married to Masilo, the son of another chief. The cattle that his father took out of his herd for the bride price for this young woman had already grazed bare the fields of her father, but still she had not seen Masilo. Only when the work on the lands was done would she see her bridegroom, for then the women of her house would take the bride, Fenya-fenyane, to the bridegroom, Masilo.

It was the duty of Fenya-fenyane to clean their home and to take care of her little brother while their mother, as it becomes a woman, worked on the lands and tilled the fields.

But he was a disobedient child, this only son of a chief. He would not listen to his sister. Every morning, when the voices of the women walking to the fields could be heard no longer, he would steal down to the river, there where Koeoko lived in the deep waters. There he would tease Koeoko, the dangerous monster, with this song:

Koeoko, Koeoko, *haba-haba*, hurry, hurry
If you can catch me

You can eat me!

And, when he was teased like this, Koeoko would jump up out of the deep waters and run after the child. But he could never catch the child, for he was heavy and clumsy, and the child was nimble on his feet, like Mutla, the rabbit.

Every day, every day that boy child did this. Just as his sister was busy sweeping inside the screen that was in front of the hut, he would slip away to the water and tease Koeoko again.

But one morning he was too slow, this boy child. Again he sang, "Koeoko, Koeoko, *haba-haba* . . . ," and the monster leaped out of the water and caught him.

Then he ate the child.

He ate the child, but he did not eat his little *karos*, his little skin blanket. That *karos* he left on the bank of the river. And then Koeoko was so full and sleepy that he lay down on the river bank and went to sleep.

When Fenya-fenyane began searching for her brother, she saw Koeoko lying there, and then she saw the *karos* of the son of her father.

Mè wheh! Mother mine! That was a sad affair! Her mother had to be told. *Mè wheh!*

She went to stand on the hill by the side of the stream and sadly she sang to the woman, far away in the fields:

> *Mè, Mè*, listen from afar,
> *Mè, Mè*, listen from afar,
> The son of our house is eaten by Koeoko,
> *Mè, Mè*, listen from afar,
> *Mè, Mè*, listen from afar.

The wind carried the sad tidings to the mother. She hushed the other women so that they could hear better what the song had to tell.

The women stopped working and leaned on their picks. They said nothing, they were quite quiet. They listened, tu-u-u-u . . .

Sadly the song came on the wind:

Mè, Mè, listen from afar,

The son of our house is eaten by Koeoko.

Yo na na oe! Oh my, oh my! It is terrible!

Then the mother of that dead child pulled the handle out of her pick and killed all the other women with it: the women who had stood so silently leaning on their picks, the women whose boy children were still living. And when they were all dead, as her child was dead, she emptied all the seeds out of her sack, emptied them all on the ground where the bodies of the dead women lay so silently.

Then she went alone to her house, and in her hand she carried the empty bag.

A bag as empty as her heart.

But along the road, as she walked, she filled the bag with scorpions, with snakes and spiders and bees and ants and other things that could bite, insects that carried poison in their teeth or in their stings.

She filled the bag with these, as her heart was filled with vengeance.

When she came to the river, she saw the *karos* of her child lying there, and beside the *karos* lay the maneater, sleeping peacefully.

Mè wheh! Mè wheh!

She picked up the *karos* of her child with the hands of love and laid it with tenderness on her own *karos* that she had spread carefully in the shade of a tree. Her heart was altogether black. Now the taking of her child had to be avenged.

The desire for vengeance took all fear out of her body and gave her strength. She tied Koeoko's feet up with ropes so that he could not get away. She tied up the monster's mouth with ropes so that he could not bite her. Then she drew her sharp knife out of its sheath and killed him.

And then the heart of the mother became quiet. And the calm

came to lie in her heart like the sunshine on the veld after a great storm had spent itself.

But her other heart remained sad. She mourned over her dead child. She mourned over her loved one that she would not see again. And the husbands and the children of the women that she had killed in the fields also mourned, for they had loved the dead women.

The whole village mourned. The whole village.

It was during this time that Fenya-fenyane had to go to the home of her bridegroom. But, because the sadness of her people was too great for any rejoicing, everyone stayed at home, and the bride had to go alone.

When she appeared in the door of her hut, arrayed in her bridal clothes and with beads around her neck, her people bade her farewell, and her mother said:

"Fenya-fenyane, do you know the way, *ná?*"

"Yes, *Mè*, I know it."

"You must look ahead only as you walk, child of mine."

"If it is your command, *Mè*, I will do it."

"You must never look back along the road you came. You must not."

"If my mother forbids it, I will obey," she promised. Then she went away from them. Alone.

She walked, she walked, she walked. As she walked all alone across the veld, she said to herself: "I must never look back. I must not." She walked along the footpath that led to her new home, with her eyes only on the road ahead of her. Just so. *Yoalo, Yoalo.*

But, as she went along a lonely part of the road, she heard footsteps following her: *shoo-shoo, shoo-shoo.*

It was something following her: *shoo-shoo, shoo-shoo.*

It came closer and closer: *shoo-shoo, shoo-shoo.*

It filled her heart with a great fear, but she did not look back. She did not do that.

When the thing reached her, it spoke. It spoke with the voice of a woman, not loudly, but soft-soft, just here by her ear: "Look back, Fenya-fenyane, look back. Behind you, from your village, thick black smoke is rising, rising straight into the air. The people of the women that your mother has killed have set fire to her hut. It is her body that is burning now, and that is where the smoke is coming from. You will never see your mother again, not even her smoke, for you will not look back."

Then Fenya-fenyane looked back, but she did not see any thick, black smoke. She saw only that strange creature that walked behind her: *shoo-shoo, shoo-shoo.* It was a woman. She was filthy, like one who searches through the ash heaps outside the village for something to eat. She wore only rags, and under the rags something horrible showed: a tail! And at the end of that tail was a greedy mouth that hunted among the bushes and grass beside the path for something to eat. Hunted. Hunted.

Mè whèh! This was evil! This monster was Moselantja, of whom the old people spoke. Fenya-fenyane knew it was she.

Then that woman with the tail again spoke soft-soft by her ear: "*Nake*, beloved, lend me your clothes, just to that place where the cattle are grazing in the long grass."

Fenya-fenyane obeyed because she was afraid. She gave her beautiful bridal dress to the creature and put on the rags of Moselantja to hide her nakedness.

When the two women reached the cattle grazing in the long grass, the one with the tail did not want to give back the beautiful clothes. She ran away quickly, straight to the village where Masilo sat waiting for the girl whom his father had exchanged for cattle and whom he had not yet seen.

But before Moselantja reached Masilo she washed herself in a little stream and took the fat that Fenya-fenyane was carrying in a little clay pot, and with it she rubbed her body and her face so that she should not look like one who had gone hungry. Then she hid the ugly tail under Fenya-fenyane's skirts, and she tied it with a rope made of grass, and then she went to Masilo. She walked modestly and quietly to the hut of the bridegroom. With a lie she told him that she was the girl that his father had exchanged for cattle. He also believed her when she slyly said to him:

"Do you see that girl in rags coming along the road? She says she is Fenya-fenyane, but it is not so. She is a creature that carries a tail under her skirts, and that creature bears the name of Moselantja." Then she spat on the ground to show her disgust.

The man believed her. He believed her, and he chased his true bride away from his village, and he threatened to set the dogs on her if she did not go away.

When Fenya-fenyane went back along her own footprints she wept so bitterly that an old woman sitting in the sweet sunlight in front of her hut felt sorry for her and called to her:

"Child of a stranger," she said, "the night is dark, and soon it will come. And when it is dark the wolves roam over the veld, and a woman dares not to be out alone. Come and sleep here with the grandmother in her hut."

Fenya-fenyane did so. She went to sleep in the hut of the old woman, but the imposter with the dreadful tail under her clothes lay with Masilo, the bridegroom.

Moselantja lay on the sleeping mat of the bridegroom. And so did the tail. But in the middle of the night the mouth at the end of the tail became very hungry. It wanted food. Then it crept out, that tail did. Softly it moved over the floor until it reached the clay pots full of food. It ate the corn porridge, it slurped the beer, and, as it fumbled among the pots, Masilo heard it and asked in the dark: "What is it that is making such a noise, wife of mine?" Moselantja quickly pulled the tail under the skin blankets and answered in a sweet voice:

"It is surely Moselantja, *Morena*, Master. You can well understand that a person with two mouths to feed will come and seek food in the hut of Masilo, where there is an abundance."

He believed her. They slept.

But when the dark became light the following morning, Masilo sent Fenya-fenyane to the fields to hoe. She had to work also, she who wore the rags.

Moselantja sat and did nothing. She sat inside the shelter of the reed screen in front of the hut, she and the tail that was so hungry. When the sun was directly overhead she said slyly:

"That poor creature in the fields is surely very hungry by now. Give me some food, and I will take it to her. My heart hurts when I think that she has to work so hard with no food inside her stomach. After all, she cannot help it that she has that tail."

Then they put some porridge for the girl in the broken clay pots out of which the dogs usually ate. But Moselantja said: "Oh, it is a disgrace! How can a person work if there is no meat in her stomach? Give her meat! Much meat!"

They gave ear to the young wife of Masilo, whose heart was so tender toward that poor creature in the fields, and they put meat with the porridge in the clay pots. Moselantja took the food and carried it on her head to the fields. But when she came to a deep ditch she sat down in it. When she had made sure that no one could see her, she let the tail come out from under her skirts and gave it the food that was meant for the real Fenya-fenyane. It ate greedily, first the meat and then the porridge. When it had finished, its mistress again lashed it to her body with a rope of grass.

Moselantja went on to the fields carrying the empty clay pots. She swung her skirts softly to and fro, just as the other women did. She walked to where Fenya-fenyane stood working. But the girl was not alone, as she had thought, for the wild doves were circling around her. Then the woman who had slept in the hut of Masilo scolded her:

"And why are you standing here while the birds are settling on the wheat? You must stand on the top of that rock so that you and your rags can frighten away the birds. And you must shout at them!

High and shrill like a colt that whinnies without stopping, so that they can fly away! You must obey me, for I am the wife of Masilo."

Then she walked back to the village. She, together with the tail that slept so quietly now under the clothes of the real bride, sleeping with satisfaction as Koeoko had also slept in satisfaction.

And the girl went and stood on top of the rock among the wheat, where the wild doves came to fly, fly, fly around her.

But she did not chase them away, she did not shout like a colt that whinnies. No, she sang to them, and in the song she told of her great humiliation:

> *Phui-i*, little doves, *phui-i, leebana,*
> Today I am called Moselantja, *phui-i, leebana,*
> Actually I am Fenya-fenyane, *phui-i, leebana,*
> I am going hungry, *phui-i, leebana.*

When she sang like that to the little doves, the *leebana*, the ears of wheat began to move, *ssss,ssss,ssss*. They bent toward her, *ssss,ssss, ssss*. Then they held her closely and bore her up in the sky to carry her back to the house of her parents. But . . . the old woman who had been sitting in the sweet sunlight beside the rock had heard everything and grabbed the feet of the girl who in reality was the bride of their chief.

"Let me go!" cried Fenya-fenyane. "I want to go back to the hut of my parents. I do not have to walk around there in the rags of that creature. Why should I work here in the fields with a cold stomach? Why should I become black with thinness and stand here on the rock with uncombed hair? Masilo prefers a bride with a tail. I want to go home!"

But the old woman held her as one holds a frightened bird and talked nicely to her. She talked nicely, she gentled her. Then the heart of Fenya-fenyane became soft, quiet as the heart of a little bird when it is afraid no longer, and she went back with the old woman to her hut. She ate of the beautiful food that the old woman gave her.

She ate unbroken boiled corn mixed with curds, she ate stew cooked from the green leaves that grow so lushly beside the dung heaps, and she ate much meat. The greasiness that remained on her hands she rubbed on her face, she took fat from the pot with her fingers and she rubbed it into her arms and legs so that they should not look so gray and neglected any more.

Her stomach was warm and yellow again, with all that food inside her. She lay down and went to sleep.

That day Masilo butchered an ox for his new wife. They cooked the meat and ate of it, and that which was left over they put in clay pots in the hut where they slept. But in the middle of the night the tail came out again from under the blankets, because all day long it had smelled the meat. Softly, softly it slid to the clay pots, the mouth went in, it ate the meat, it slurped the gravy. But it was so greedy that it did not eat quietly. As it burrowed into the pots Masilo awoke. He said: "What is it that makes so much noise, wife of mine?"

And she answered: "It is surely again the girl with the two mouths, *Morena*. She must have come after the smell of the meat. But now she has gone again."

He said that he would chase her away from the village the next day. Then they slept.

But the next morning the old woman came to Masilo and persuaded him to go to the fields with her, along the path that led through the tall grass. He was bent double as he walked, and he sat down with the old woman among the wheat beside the big rock, and they waited. It was the command of an old person, and Masilo obeyed.

They did not see the girl dressed in rags, they only heard how beautifully she sang to the birds. Later in the day they saw the bride coming, but they did not see the tail. It slept quietly around the body of its mistress, for again she had stopped in the ditch and the mouth had eaten all the food, the food that was meant for the girl. No,

Moselantja did not give the girl any food. She scolded her and said:

"Why do you sleep when you have to chase the birds away? I told you that you have to stand on the rock so that your rags can scare the birds away. I said you had to whinny high and shrill like a colt, so that the birds should fly away. You must listen when I command!"

Because the woman spoke with the authority that she had appropriated for herself as the wife of Masilo, Fenya obeyed. She climbed on to the top of the rock and gave high, shrill cries like a colt whinnying. It chased her companions, the *leebana*, away from her, but as soon as Moselantja was out of earshot she enticed the birds to her again with the sad song: *Phui-i, leebana, phui-i, little doves. . . .*

Then the ears of the wheat began to quiver again, *ssss*. They bent toward her again, *ssss*. They again held her closely and drew her up into the air, just as they had done the day before. But Masilo held her around the body, and he held her so tightly that the wheat had to let her go. And it was the first time that he saw how beautiful was the girl who said she was Fenya-fenyane, the woman who really belonged to him. Because now that the doves and the wheat believed her, he had to believe her also.

And, after the old one told him the true story of the two women, his heart was so sore that he wept. When he had finished weeping, he sat there in the sweet sunlight and thought of a plan to kill the evil one. When he had finished thinking he got up and walked home. He said nothing, for it does not become a man to open his heart in front of a woman.

When the dark of the night became light again the following day, he sent the women of the village, and also Fenya-fenyane, to fetch dry kindling from the mountains. While they were gone, he and the men dug a big hole, they dug a big hole and in the bottom they put much food, as one puts food in the grave of one who has died: meat, sour porridge, beer, buttermilk together with the butter that had been churned out of it, and a calabash full of sweet milk. Then they covered the hole with reeds. On top of the reeds they scattered a thin layer of soil and loose grass. Then they waited for the young women to return with the kindling.

Now, these women. Each one gathered dry kindling for herself, just enough for a bundle that could be carried on her head, and as each one gathered enough she tied it tightly with a grass rope that she had brought along for that purpose. But when they wanted to go home, they saw that the wife of Masilo was not with them.

It was great trouble! The daughter-in-law of the chief! *Yo, yo!*

They began to search. They called, but she did not answer. She did not answer even though she heard them, for she did not want them to come to her. They must not know that she quickly took the tail with its incessant hunger to the stream, where its greedy mouth could hunt for crabs and frogs in the shallow water.

Later, when she heard the sound of calling voices coming closer, she quickly put the tail under her skirts again. She did not have time to tie the tail with the grass rope, for she still had to find enough kindling for her bundle. But here by the water there was no kindling, so she quickly pulled a bunch of green reeds from the ground, put them on her head, and went to meet the other women.

When she saw Fenya-fenyane's bundle of dry, black wood she snatched it from her head and forced Fenya to carry the miserable little bundle of green reeds back to the village, in shame.

When they reached the village, Masilo called them. He said: "You women, put the bundles down on the ground, and one by one you come here and jump over this place where the loose soil is scattered. But that wife of mine must jump last of all, only when she has seen that all of you have jumped over safely."

They obeyed him. They jumped over the loose soil, *tlutla, tlutla, tlutla!* Everybody jumped over, Fenya also. But when Moselantja jumped over, the tail caught the smell of the good food in the bottom of the hole, the food that its mistress, the woman, did not even know about. Just as its mistress jumped, it shot out because it was not fastened with the rope. It dived into the hole and pulled the woman down into it, down into the hole that was like a grave.

Yo na na oe! What a terrible thing! Everybody saw the tail before the woman disappeared into the hole.

And while Masilo told all the people of the village who were assembled there about the deception of Moselantja, Fenya-fenyane sat aside demurely looking at the ground, as it becomes a young bride.

The men threw more soil on the body in the hole. They buried her with the tail and the good food.

Now the heart of Fenya-fenyane was very happy. She laughed, she sang, she washed her body in fresh water until it was clean. She rubbed her face with fat until it shone, she combed her hair. Then they gave her beautiful clothes to wear, they gave her beads and rings to adorn her body. She became the wife of Masilo and they had a child, a boy child.

When this child was made loose from the maternity hut in his third month, as was the custom, his young mother carried him in the carrying skin on her back to the fields where the women hoed the weeds. One day she arrived there and saw a big bitter melon rolling toward her.

It was a strange thing!

Yo, this melon spoke like a person!

Yo, it was the voice of a woman, of Moselantja! It said, *"Pi-ti-ki, pi-ti-ki,* we eat the food of the fat young mother, the wife of Masilo."

Fenya was very scared. Listen how that thing without even a mouth says " *'pi-ti-ki, pi-ti-ki.'* Lay the child of my husband on the ground." She did so, and, as soon as the little one was no longer on her back, that melon jumped up in the air and knocked Fenya down. And then it rolled, rolled, rolled away again.

From that day onward this thing happened to the mother of Masilo's child every day when she went to the fields. The melon came rolling toward her, *pi-ti-ki, pi-ti-ki,* it knocked her down, *pi-ti-ki, pi-ti-ki,* then rolled away, *pi-ti-ki, pi-ti-ki.*

Just like that. *Yoalo, yoalo.*

Masilo one day noticed that his pretty young wife was getting thin. She grew black in the face, and he asked her what was biting her. Then she told him of the melon that spoke with the voice of Moselantja. Then they knew it was the woman with the tail who had risen from the ground in the form of that melon.

Now he, the father of the child, had to fight the danger that threatened the mother of the child. He went with his wife to the fields and hid behind the sleeping mat of the child. The melon came rolling *pi-ti-ki, pi-ti-ki,* and he heard the voice of Moselantja, "*Pi-ti-ki,* we eat the food of the fat young mother, the wife of Masilo."

But when the melon rose in the air to knock down his wife, he jumped from his hiding place with his battle axe in his hand and aimed it at that strange thing that wanted to assault his wife.

He hit, and, where he hit the melon with his axe, blood flowed out, as though it were a wound on the body of a person.

Masilo doubted no longer, it was Moselantja. He chopped the melon in little pieces and burned them in the fire until they were ashes.

But where the ashes were thrown, thorns grew. They spread and spread, and all over the footpaths were little thorns that hurt the feet of the child of Masilo.

Then Masilo said that all the little thorns had to be gathered, and he burned them all in the big fires that he commanded to be lit in front of his hut.

But when the thorns burned it was only the body of the creature that was being destroyed, her spirit was changed into insects and biting animals that crept into the dung floor of the chief's hut and hid in the thatch of the roof. Then at night they all came to the child of the chief and bit him so that he could not sleep.

It was Moselantja who was sucking his blood with the mouths of the insects.

But for this Masilo also had a plan. He told them to take the child out of the hut, completely naked, and then he set the thatched roof on fire. It burned out, the plaster on the walls burned out, and the dung floor blistered from the heat, and everything in the hut was destroyed. Not only all the clothes, the skin blankets, and the sleeping mats, but also the insects, they who were the heart of Moselantja.

So this is the end of the story of the woman with the terrible tail.

Ke tsomo ka mathetho, which means, this is a true tale of the Basotho people.

5. Hen, Hawk, and the Needle

This is a story that is told by the old people. They had heard it from the parents of their parents.

They said Hawk and Hen were very great friends in the days when birds could talk. Every day, every day Hawk came down to the ground to listen to the cheerful conversation of his friend. *Auk,* that woman could talk well! She could laugh! It was *kêkêkê, kêkêkê,* all the time she talked. *Yo,* Hawk loved that woman a lot!

But he was the only bird who owned a needle, and one day Hen asked him, "Friend of mine, please lend me your needle."

Hawk was very careful of his needle, so he asked first, "What do you want to do with it?"

"I have some beautiful little skins that I have kept for a long time. If only I had a needle I could sew them together and make a beautiful blanket."

"Friend of mine," said Hawk. "*Chè,* because I love you so much I will lend it to you, but you must take very good care of it."

"I will take as good care of it as I do of my children. I will use it carefully, and, when I have finished the blanket, I will give it back to you immediately. Truly, I will do so."

"But it could happen that you lose it. A needle is easily lost. And if it happens, how can I do my work?" asked Hawk.

"*Kêkêkê*," she laughed. "You need not be afraid. If I have an accident and cannot give you back your needle, you may catch one of my chicks and eat it."

"*Chè*, that is a good idea!"

Now Hawk was satisfied. He flew away and fetched the needle from where he always kept it and brought it to Hen.

Yo, that woman was glad! She took all the little skins that she had tanned so carefully until they were beautifully soft and put them on the ground beside her. Then she sewed them together with the needle of her good friend. She made a beautiful blanket for herself, a *hlosi*, the kind of skin blanket that only a chief or one of his big wives may wear.

When she had finished, she hung it round her shoulders. She paraded in front of her children, and her heart felt good when they said: "*Au mè*, you are beautiful! More beautiful than all the other women!"

She walked outside, she shot her little legs out as she walked, she wiggled her body, and she walked up and down in front of her house, like the wife of a chief, and her heart felt good when she heard the strange chickens say: "*Yo*, she shines, that woman! You can see her husband is a chief!"

Her head was so full of these flattering things that she never gave a thought to the needle of Hawk. She quite forgot that she had left it on the floor of her house.

Yo...yo...yo...

When she had shown her skin blanket to everyone in the village, she called her chicks and said: "My beloved little ones, go and tidy the house for me. Sweep it well. Pick up the dirt and throw it on the ash heaps. A woman with such a beautiful skin blanket must not tread on such a dirty floor."

Then she walked, *shoo-shoo-shoo*, to the lands, so that the hens who were hoeing could see how beautiful she was.

The chicks swept the house, just as she had said. Just so. *Yoalo.* They picked up the dirt, they went to throw it on the ash heaps, just as their mother wanted it. Just so. *Yoalo.*

And . . . among the dirt was the needle of Hawk, but they did not know it. They did not know it. They did not know it. Not know it!

All the women on the lands also told Hen how beautiful she looked in the blanket, and, when she walked home late that afternoon as though she were the wife of a chief, she did not think of the words of the old people when they say that deep pools of water can also dry up, meaning that a proud person can also suffer disgrace. She did not think of it, but still—it can happen. It can, because overhead Hawk was circling between her and the sun. His shadow fell on her path, and he called to her from the sky:

"*Yo, yo,* wife of a chief, you have a high opinion of yourself in that blanket, isn't that so?"

Ekkê, the hen cackled. *Ekkê!* But she did not look up. Then Hawk cried: "Friend of mine, give me my needle now, so that I can put it away safely again."

And for the first time Hen thought of the needle! She jumped with fright and did not answer, but scurried back to her straw hut.

Yo, when she came inside she trod on a floor that had been swept clean. She looked round, but there was nothing on the floor. The needle was gone.

Yo, she thought, it is surely lying on the ash heaps among the dirt that the children threw away. *Yo, yo!*

As fast as she could she ran to the ash heaps, but as she ran she could see the black shadow of Hawk sliding over the ground alongside her, and it became black inside her also, for she knew what

Hawk wanted: his needle, or one of the children that she loved so much.

When she came to the ash heaps she wasn't even wearing the blanket any more. She had lost it, but she did not care, all she wanted was to hunt for that needle.

She scratched, they searched, but they did not find it.

Hawk saw them searching and knew that they were searching for his needle. When he saw that they had not found it, he dived down to the ground to snatch a chick, but the eye of the mother saw him and she groaned, MMMMMMM! as though she were in great pain.

Her children heard her cry, and they came running and crept under the wings that she spread open for them.

She groaned loudly, but they sat quite still. *Tu-u-u-u.*

When Hawk had gone, they came out fearfully and began their search again.

There was unrest in the heart of that mother. Unrest and fear. She had completely forgotten about the beautiful blanket. She only thought of the needle, of the hawk, and of her children.

For a little while she had been like the wife of a chief, now she was again only a mother whose beloved children were in danger. She must find that needle! She must search, she must not stop!

The other hens came to see what she and her chicks were doing. They asked what was going on. She told them of the great unrest in her heart, and they understood. They were sorry for her, very sorry, because they also had children. They also had hearts.

Now everybody helped her to search. Their chicks helped also, but they could not find that needle.

And, as the shadow of the hawk slid over the earth, the mothers would groan as though they were in great pain, and then the children would come and take cover under the wings of their mothers, until the danger was over. And then they would begin to search, search, search again.

But they never found that needle again.

It was gone. Altogether gone. To this day.

And in the place of that needle came unrest. Unrest and fear. *Yoalo, yoalo.* Unrest and fear.

And here the story comes to an end.

6. Roaqo, the Woman Who Ate People

The old people tell of Masilo, who was the son of a chief. He married a woman who was a witch. She was very bad-tempered and scolded Masilo all day long. Scolded and argued. But he always kept quiet, kept quiet.

But one day her heart was very black, and she took a stick and wanted to hit him. Then he called his dogs and went away from that woman. He and his dogs.

He walked, he walked, he walked until he came to the top of a high mountain. He looked down and saw a big basin in the mountains and to one side a village with many huts standing among the cotton trees. He saw many oxen grazing in the long grass, but there were no herders whistling to them. He saw many goats and sheep, but no boy children walking behind the herds.

Chè, this was strange!

What kind of people could these be? There was no one tilling the ground, tilling the fields that he saw among the bushes, there was no grain growing or pumpkins lying on the ground. He saw no women working there.

Chè, it must be very strange people who lived like this!

It must be a strong tribe who owned this region, he thought, for the village was big.

There were many huts, but no people tending fires, and he saw no smoke lying on the village like a cloud. He saw only one little smoke curling blue against the sky.

This was something that Masilo could not understand at all. He knew of no people who lived like this, and he was eager to see them.

Then he stood up. He called to his dogs and went down the mountain to see what kind of people lived in that village. He walked cautiously, for he was afraid that they might attack him. He called to his dogs that they should stay right behind him. He kept to the bushes, and he slowly came nearer to the village. And when he came to the ash heaps he saw something that completely stunned him: there were many ash heaps, but no hens walked around on them, surrounded by their chicks. He had never seen an ash heap where the hens and the chicks were not searching for the needle of the hawk, as the old story tells.

No, he had never seen people who had no chickens. He crept warily toward the huts, for he was afraid that the dogs would fly at him. At last he was among the huts, but there were no dogs growling around him either. *Chè*, they must have gone to the veld with the men to hunt rabbits, so he thought. But still he wondered just where the men were hunting. He had not seen a single one.

He did not see children playing around the huts either. If they had gone to the mountains to pick berries he would have seen them, he thought. On the fields he had seen no women, and here, too, were no women. Not even an old woman sitting in the sweet sunlight to get warm.

He saw that the whole village was deserted. There was nothing that lived. There were no chickens, there were no dogs, there were no children, there were no grownups. There were no old people.

He was afraid to be the only creature alive in the middle of such desolation. He wanted to leave quickly. He called to his dogs, and, when they began to run, the smell of smoke came to his nostrils. Then he remembered the one little blue smoke that he had seen from the mountain top. He hunted for the hut that had a fire burning. And when he found it he cautiously peeped around the reed screen in front of the hut.

There he saw a human being sitting by the fire. It was a young girl! *Yo*, but she was beautiful!

But she was sad in her loneliness and was startled when he greeted her, "*Lumele*, my sister."

But she answered him respectfully: "*Lumele*, my big brother."

He asked: "What is the reason that you live alone in this village, from which everything living has fled? Why is it that there is smoke coming from only this one hut?"

Then she replied: "Roaqo is the reason. She is my mother. And you, stranger, you must go away quickly, for she will return soon."

"*Ná*, what is wrong with your mother, sister of mine?"

"She eats people. She is a *limo*, a maneater. Everyone who used to live here lies buried in her stomach. The chickens also, the cats and the dogs also. She will eat you too. Your dogs also."

Masilo said that he would leave, but that she must come with him. She said it was right, she would do so. But, just as they came out of the entrance in the reed screen, she saw the pickaxe of her mother shining in the sun. It was the pickaxe with which she killed people.

Then they quietly slipped back inside the screen. The young woman quickly grabbed another axe that was lying there and dug a hole in the floor of her hut. She dug, she dug, she dug until that hole was big enough for Masilo and his dogs. She hid them in the hole, then she laid a flat stone over the opening, and over the stone she spread a sleeping mat, so that her mother should not know that a human being and his dogs were hidden in the hole.

But the moment Roaqo put her foot inside the screen she said: "I smell a human. I smell a dog."

Her daughter asked: "Where is the human? Where is the dog?"

Chè, Roaqo did not know where the human was, where the dog was. She went to sit down inside the screen's shelter, but she kept on saying: "I smell a human. I smell a dog. The skin of my stomach is black because there is no meat inside it."

Then the girl wept. She said: "The only human that you smell is myself. Do you want to eat me also, as you ate my father?"

But the mother replied: "*Chè*, I am very hungry, but my child I cannot eat. My child was part of myself. How can I eat my own body?"

Then she went to sleep, that maneater. But when the dark of the night became light the next day, she got up. She tied up her hungry belly with a leather thong, and then she went out again to hunt for meat.

She carried her shining pickaxe over her shoulder.

She walked, she walked, she walked until she came to a field where three young girls were pulling weeds from among the corn. She was very glad when she saw them. She spoke to them. With a lie she said: "Your parents have sent me to call you, my children."

They believed, for was she not grown up? But the moment they came to a creek she quickly killed all three of them. And she ate one. She ate quickly, for the meat was tender.

But she was not yet satisfied.

And so she ate the second one. Then she ate the third one also. Then she talked to herself: "*Ha*, the stomach of this old woman is nice and warm now. It is yellow, but she does not know where she will find more food, for on this earth there are no people left any more." Then she went to lie down in the creek.

She lay in the water like a dog that feels the heat, and she went to sleep. When she woke up the sun had already set, but she was

not afraid. She was not afraid at all, for she thought that there was
no creature on earth that would want to eat an old maneater.

But as she walked in the dark, she saw a wild animal stalking
her. She was very frightened, but she made a plan. She said to it:
"Let us run a race. The one who wins can eat the other one."

So they made a bargain. Then they ran, but Roaqo could not out-
strip the creature. He won, he won, he won completely! But just as
he wanted to eat her, she said: "My friend, leave me. Leave me,
and I will fetch ten fat cows for you from my corral. Ten cows are
worth more than one old woman whose flesh is tough and stringy."

The creature was satified. So they made a new bargain. He
waited there for her, and she went to fetch the cows. But she did
not bring him any cows—she went to her home where her daughter
lived alone.

But again, as she set foot inside the shelter she said: "I smell a
human. I smell a dog. I am hungry."

But her daughter wept and said her mother must want to eat her
for she was the only creature there that smelled like a human.
Again her mother convinced her that a maneater would never eat
its own child, for your child is part of yourself, and how can you
want to eat your own body?

Then she slept. That *limo*.

But when the dark grew light she was even hungrier. She pulled
the leather thong tighter around her empty stomach, she shouldered
her pickaxe and went out again to search for people that she could
eat.

But she did not go in the direction of the wild animal that sat
waiting for its ten fat cows. She went in quite another direction.

She walked, she walked, she walked. She walked for many days
and for many nights, searching for food. She ate the little frogs and
crabs that she found in the creeks, and they kept her alive.

And while she was gone, Masilo took the daughter of the maneater as a wife, and they had a child. They were very happy, until

one day they again saw the pickaxe of Roaqo glistening in the sun. Her daughter knew that the *limo* was returning, and she hid the child together with his father and the dogs in a hole and covered it with mats.

As soon as that *limo* set her foot inside the screen, she said: "I smell a human. I smell a dog. I smell an infant. I smell mother's milk." And in anger she went out of the hut to seek out that human, that dog, that infant, that mother's milk.

She searched and she searched. She searched through the deserted village, and when she found nothing she went out of the village to search through the veld.

As soon as Roaqo was out of sight her daughter took the mats from the hole in which her husband had hidden together with their child and the dogs. She loaded all their possessions on a few pack oxen: blankets made of jackal skin, blankets made of cowskin, blankets made of sheepskin, and blankets made of the skins of many little furry animals. Then the young mother bound the infant on her back in the *thari*, the skin blanket for carrying babies. And then she and Masilo and the big herd of oxen fled from that deserted village of the *limo*.

They fled, they fled, they fled, and the dogs ran with them.

They had already gone a long way when a dangerous snake barred their way. It barred their way. And Masilo immediately knew that it was a thing that his first wife had put in their way to keep them from her house. But the dogs of Masilo killed that snake. Then the road was open again so that he, his wife, and their infant, and also the big herd of oxen and the dogs could go on their way.

They walked until they reached the top of a hill, and when they looked back they saw something shining in the sun.

It was the pickaxe of Roaqo. When they saw it, they knew that she was following their scent, and they were afraid, for they knew then that the man and the child would find their graves in her stomach.

But the dogs attacked her when she came near. They attacked her and they killed her. And when the danger of the maneater was gone, as the danger of the snake was gone, they went on their way again.

With calm in their hearts they reached the place where the oxen of the father of Masilo were herded, where they grazed so that they would not harm the crops in the fields.

And there they settled, Masilo and his wife and their child, and he tended the cattle on the mountainsides. He tended their own herd and he tended the herds of his father.

And from there he sent a message to his father, the chief. He told him that he had taken a second wife and that they had a boy child and that they should build a hut for the new wife, so that she could move into that hut when he brought her to the home of his people.

When the wife of the chief built the new hut for her second daughter-in-law and erected the reed screen in front of it, that first wife of Masilo saw it and her heart grew black with hate.

But this woman was a witch. Her witchcraft would help her against Masilo and the hated second wife.

When the second wife and the child came to live in the new hut, the witch came to thank her for the child, as was the custom among the people. She picked the little one up, and as she held him she put a spell on him, without the mother knowing it.

That night he started to cry. And he cried, and he cried, he cried until he died.

And the second child that was later born to the wife of Masilo died also, just so. Just so. And the third one also. Just so. Just so.

The grief of the unhappy parents was terrible. And when two girl children were born, the mother did not want to stay there where her children could not live. They went back to that village where they had lived with her mother, Roaqo.

It was so far away, thought she, that the evil powers of that first wife could not reach her little girl children. And there they grew up nicely.

But one day when they were playing outside, they saw two chickens on the ash heaps outside the village. It was something they had never seen at all. They ran to the two pretty birds, but the chickens ran farther and farther away from the village of Roaqo.

Farther and farther.

Farther and farther, and the little girls ran after them. Later the parents began to search for their children. They followed the footprints that the little girls had left in the sand, with the little footprints of the chickens beside them, but they never found the children again.

Masilo knew that it was his first wife's doing. He went to report the matter to his father. The chief called all the men together in a *khotla*, the ceremonial gathering of the tribesmen, and the witch-woman was called to appear before them and tell them why she had done these deeds.

The verdict of the *khotla* was that she had to sacrifice her own life to atone for the murders that she had committed. The head man of the chief put her to death, and after she was dead that second wife of Masilo had many more children.

They did not die.

They grew up.

They married and had children.

These children, their children, and their children's children filled all the huts of the village that had stood empty, that had stood empty after Roaqo had eaten all the people.

And here the story comes to an end.

7. Tortoise and Dove

It was in the days of the big hunger. There was a big famine in the land, and Tortoise had no more food left to eat. He walked around the little bushes and hunted, hunted, hunted around for something to put inside his stomach. He hunted, but he found nothing. And so he pulled his head and his little legs under his shell, for he was afraid he might die of hunger.

Now Tortoise is a man who always walks alone. He has no father or mother to take care of him. He has no wife or children who can work for him. So now he would have to die alone, he thought. He lay down with his hungry stomach. *Tu-u-u-u*.

Dove, who sat high up in a tree, saw how Tortoise was hunting for food. She also saw that he found nothing. Nothing at all. And she felt very sorry for him when she saw him lying there so quietly. She sang to him: *Coor-coor, coor-coor*, but he did not put his head out of his shell.

"Tortoise, big man, why don't you go to the other side of the river? I fly there every day, and there is plenty of food."

Tortoise stuck his head out from under his shell and listened to what Dove had to say.

"Keep quiet, woman!" he shouted. "How can that food help me if there is a stream of water between me and the food?"

"But you can swim through, big man," she said.

"I am not a fish that I can swim," said Tortoise.

"Why don't you fly over the river?"

"Because I am not a bird. Where are my wings?"

Tortoise wept over the plentiful food on the other side of the river. He wept because he was so hungry he was afraid he might die.

Dove wept with him. *Coor-coor, coor-coor, coor-coor!*

Then she had a plan.

"Tortoise," she said. "Find a dry stick, and bite on one end."

"I don't eat sticks, Mother," said Tortoise sadly.

"It is not for you to eat," said Dove. "I will take the other end of the stick in my mouth and fly over the water with you."

"That is a fine plan, Mother," said Tortoise.

"Yes, it is a fine plan," agreed Dove. "But you must not talk to Fish if he rises from the water to talk to you."

"No, I will not," Tortoise promised.

And then they did as they had planned. *Yoalo, yoalo.* Tortoise found a dry stick and bit on one end, and Dove bit on the other end, and they flew out over the water. Dove flew over the water, and Tortoise hung below her on the other end of the stick.

Au, but that was a strange business! Fish could not believe what he saw. He looked, he looked, he looked, but he could not understand it at all. He was astonished, for he had never in his life seen a tortoise high up in the sky.

"You, fellow," said Fish, with his mouth full of water. "I never knew that you could fly! If I did not see this with my own eyes, I would not believe it!"

Tortoise became angry with Fish.

"What do you think?" he asked. "And why should I not be able
to fly?"

But before he could finish speaking he fell *twaaah!* right into the
water. He had let go of the stick when he argued with Fish, and
Dove flew away with only the stick in her mouth.

She came back again to see whether Tortoise would come out of
the water. She flew to and fro over the water to see whether Tortoise might come out higher upstream, or whether he might come
out of the water lower downstream. But no, there was no sign of
him. She kept on flying, she kept on flying with the stick in her
mouth, but to no avail. Tortoise stayed under the water. He did
not come up again.

Then she went to lay the little stick down on her nest. But her
heart remained black, it would not lie down, because of the big man
who had fallen in the water. She wept over him: *Coor-coor, coor-
coor, coor-coor* . . .

Every day. Every day. Until this very day.

And she keeps on hunting for Tortoise. She keeps the stick in her
mouth. She wants to give it to Tortoise again so that she can lift
him out of the water as soon as he shows his head.

But Tortoise will never come out of the water again. No, he will
not, because he found plenty of food under the water on the river
bed. Much more food than there ever was on the ground and under
the trees. He will never come out of the water again. He will stay
there.

And this is how Tortoise became Turtle. And here the story
comes to an end.

8. The Guilty Woman

This is the story of a man who was very rich. He had so much cattle that he could barter them for more wives than any other man—if the chief is not counted. No, he was a very wealthy man.

One day he went to hunt, but he was very unlucky. He brought no game back to his village. All that he could find was a tortoise. He took it to his first wife and asked her to cook it for him, for the hunger had caught him.

But that big wife said: "*H-ha*, I do not cook such things as tortoises! Give that sort of work to one of your other wives!"

Then he went to the second one, and she also said: *H-ha*, she did not cook tortoises. Then he went to the third one, the fourth one, and all the others, but they all said *h-ha*, they would not cook such a thing as a tortoise.

But the youngest one, she who was the littlest one, said: "No, that will be good, Father. I shall cook it for you."

Then she cooked the tortoise. She cooked it, she cooked it, and, when it was tender and done, she dished it up in a little clay bowl, together with the gravy, and she covered it with a little grass mat so that the dogs and the cats could not get at it. And, after she had put it on a low wall outside the hut, she went to the veld to gather broom grass.

That afternoon, when she came home, the husband was sitting by the fire and asked: "Little wife, where were you for such a long time? I told you I was very hungry. Bring me meat so that I can eat."

"Here it is, Big Man," said she, and gave him the dish with the little grass mat over it. He took it. *Yoalo. Yoalo. Yoalo.*

He laughed when he took it, and he smacked his lips. But when he looked inside, he saw that there was no meat in that dish, and no gravy either. Everything had been eaten up. Only the shell of the tortoise lay in the dish.

Yo, he was cross with that wife!

"You have eaten it!" he shouted at her, for the skin on his stomach was black with hunger.

"It is not I who ate it, Grandfather," she said. "It is the truth that I speak. I did not eat it. Not at all. It is also not a dog or a cat that ate it, for I put it in a safe place, and it was well covered with the little grass mat, as you saw for yourself."

But the hunger and the yearning for the meat made him quite crazy. He did not want to believe her. He said: "I am going to the witch doctor right now. His magic bones will speak and tell me whether it was you who ate my meat. Then I shall know."

Then he went. He went, and when he came there he and the owner of those magic bones talked for a long while about the payment. They talked, talked, talked until the magic bones and the magic stones were satisfied with the price. Then they told the witch doctor that they were willing to tell the stranger what he wanted to know.

Then the witch doctor once more scattered the bones and the

stones in front of him on the ground, and they spoke to him as tea leaves speak to some people.

Everything that the stones and the bones said, their master repeated word for word to the man. They could not tell him who had taken the meat, but they gave him a good plan to find out who it had been.

He went home and did as those magic bones and stones had told him to do.

He took a long thong that had been plaited from the sinews of a kudu. He took it to the deep pool in the river, and he took all the people of his village with him, the men and the women and the children. His own wives and their children also. That was what the bones had told him to do.

When they reached the pool, he gave that rope of sinews to the two strongest men and said: "One must stand on this side and hold one end of the rope. The other must take the other end and go and stand on the other side of the pool."

That was what the magic bones of the clever man had said. And the two men did just so. *Yoalo. Yoalo. Yoalo.*

They spanned a bridge over the pool with that rope of sinews, and, when they had done so, the man called his littlest wife, she who had cooked the tortoise. He commanded her:

"You go and walk over the water on that rope. From this side to that side. If the kudu's sinews snap and you fall in the water, all the people here will know it was you who ate the meat that was meant for me, and drank the gravy that was meant for me. If the rope does not break, everybody will know that you are innocent."

The little wife did as the man had commanded her. She trod on the rope, she trod, she trod, and then she walked. Very carefully. Below her the water went *shoo-shoo, shoo-shoo,* but she walked. She walked, and as she walked she sang:

Sinews of kudu, break . . . that I might fall,

That in the water I might fall ... that I might fall,
They say I ate the tortoise ... that I might fall,
But tortoise I did not eat ... that I might fall ...

She walked. She sang. She walked. She sang. She walked, but the sinews did not break; they carried her to the other side of the dark pool of water, in safety.

Then everybody knew that she was innocent. It was not she who had eaten the tortoise meat.

Now another wife had to walk over the water, on the thin rope plaited of kudu sinews. When this wife walked, she also sang the same song that the little one had sung:

Sinews of kudu, break ... that I might fall,
That in the water I might fall ... that I might fall,
Yoalo, yoalo, yoalo ...

But the sinews did not break. They did not break at all, but carried her safely to the other side of the water. And everybody saw that she was innocent. *Hm*, it was a strange business!

And so the man called all his wives who sat there waiting for their turn to walk over the water on that rope. And everyone who walked sang the same song:

Sinews of kudu, break ... that I might fall,
Yoalo, that I might fall, *yoalo, yoalo,*
Sinews of kudu, break ... that I might fall ...

But the sinews did not break. They stayed whole, and carried every wife, one after the other, to safety. *Yoalo. Yoalo.*

But then they came to the last one, the big wife who had been the first to refuse to cook the tortoise for their husband.

"Now it is your turn, Mother," he said to her.

Then she stood up and trod on that rope, as the others had done. One foot in front of the other. Cautiously, cautiously. And as she walked, she sang the song that all the others had sung:

Sinews of kudu, break ... that I might fall,
That in the water I might fall ... that I might fall,

They say I ate the tortoise . . . that I might fall,

But tortoise I did not eat . . . that I might fall . . .

Just so. *Yoalo.*

She walked, one foot in front of the other. One foot in front of the other, but when she came to the middle of that deep, dark pool the rope broke. It broke, and *twaaah!* the big wife fell into the water. Before everybody's eyes she disappeared in the depths of that water.

Then everybody knew it was she who had eaten the meat of the tortoise and had drunk the gravy. And they saw how she was punished by drowning.

No, it is right so, said everybody as they walked home. The old people say that you must stoop when you come to your own possessions, but when you come to those of others you must stand up straight. Which means that you must keep your hands off that which belongs to other people.

Now, that big wife had stooped when she came to her husband's food, she took it, and she ate it. But the magic bones had made a good plan. So they had spoken, and so it had happened. No, it was right so.

And this is the end of the story.

9. Monyohe, the Great Snake of the Deep Waters

The old people tell of a chief who married a woman who was a *nyopa*. She was a *nyopa*, a woman who had no children. It caused him great sorrow, for the huts of the least among his subjects were full of children in the evenings, boy children and girl children. But he, the big chief, did not even have one child who could sit beside the fire with him and his wife.

Then they went to ask the advice of a witch doctor. This man was the cleverest of all the witch doctors in the region. He said *chè*, he could take away the barrenness from the woman. She will have a boy child, but his body will not be like that of a human being, for it will be wrapped in the skin of the water serpent.

So it happened. Just so. *Yoalo.*

The chief was very grateful that the sorrow of childlessness was lifted from them, and they loved that child that was covered with the shining scales of the water snake. They loved him, but still they were ashamed if other people saw him. They hid him in the darkness of their hut. On top of the walls, just below the place where the grass roof rested, their son slept during the day and during the night. Here he grew up, and no one ever saw him. Nobody except his father and his mother.

The parents never made a fire in the hut, for the smoke would blind the child whom they called Monyohe. At night they went to bed without light, or they used the flame from a little fat that they poured on a smoldering piece of dung, which they had put in a broken clay pot. But they loved their child very much, the child Monyohe, who was a snake.

Ghillick! That child was clever! He could speak. He could sing. He could dance. And he could eat so much—more than three grown men could eat! He ate meat, he ate corn porridge, he drank beer. All kinds of food, just like a human being. And he grew quickly, he grew so big that he filled the hut of his parents right to the roof when he curled, curled, curled his long body in a heap on the floor.

At last his mother had to build a special hut for him next to their own home. All the subjects of the chief were curious to see that wonderful child, and they thought it would happen when the big man walked from the hut of his parents to his own hut.

But it did not happen. No, it did not happen.

When they had finished thatching the roof of Monyohe's new hut, the parents waited until the middle of the night, when everybody was asleep. Then Monyohe slid from the hut of his parents to his own hut. He slid, slid, slid, and when he was inside his own hut he curled up, curled up, curled up in a heap that became so big that it nearly filled the whole room.

Then he slept.

When the time came that this son of the chief had to go to the school of grass huts in order to be initiated with the other boys of the tribe, the school where the boys learn wisdom from the old men, his father made a grass hut for him, far away from the huts of the other boys. The people all thought that now they would see this son of the chief, but it did not happen. In the night, the night that would hide the humiliation of the parents, Monyohe slid to that grass hut where he had to live for five months, as the other young men lived in the other grass huts of the school. And at the end of the five months his father also fetched him in the middle of the night. Then he set the hut on fire, according to the traditions of the tribe.

But that night, when the young men of the tribe feasted to celebrate their "loosening" from the grass hut school, the son of the chief was not with them. He did not eat with them, he did not drink with them, he did not dance with them!

The tribe was filled with wonder about this mysterious son of their chief. They shook their heads. *Tu* . . .

When the young man had finished with the *bolla*, the initiation school, his father said to him: "Monyohe, son of my house, the time has come that I must find a wife for you. My thoughts go to the daughter of the chief who lives to the east of the mountains. My corrals are full of cattle, and my herds of sheep and goats cover the mountainside where they graze. I shall take out many, many heads of cattle for the girl, because I have no other sons for whose brides I have to barter cattle."

But Monyohe was not at all satisfied with this. He said: "Father of mine, it is not you who will choose a wife for me. I myself will have to do that."

His father was upset as he replied: "That will be very unwise of you, Monyohe, *thlè*. When the girls see your form they will not want to come near to you! I shall have to set a trap for them. And it must be done in such a manner that the girl and her mother must not know of it. You must leave the matter in my hands, big man!"

But Monyohe was very stubborn and insisted that it would be he himself who would choose a wife. He, Monyohe, and no one else.

That night he slid to the pool where the daughters of the other chief always came to bathe. He went to that pool, and when he came there he went to a rock overhanging the pool, and in the waters beneath that rock Monyohe waited. Monyohe waited. He waited. He waited.

The next day the girls came to bathe. Monyohe watched them through the green waters as they played in the water. He saw them all, and he studied them all well. Very well. And he chose Senkepeng, the only daughter of the big wife of the chief.

At once Monyohe wanted to join in the games of the girls, but, when they saw his scales shining through the water and felt his cold body touching theirs, they knew it was the great danger of the deep waters. *Yo wheh!* they screamed and fled as quickly as they could.

But Monyohe called to Senkepeng to come back, and, when she stood fearlessly on the banks of the pool, he said: "Senkepeng, *moratua*—beloved—how can you run away from love itself? For you are the one I have chosen from all the girls of the land to be my wife!"

But she laughed at him. She laughed at the snake who had let his eye fall with love on the proud daughter of the great chief. Mockingly she asked: "With what will you pay for a wife? Show me where your cattle are grazing."

And he replied: "*Chè*, I have water!"

"Water? *Yo!*"

Then she laughed at him again and said that he had no arms, so how could he protect a wife? He did not have legs, so how could he dance with her? Just so! *Yoalo!*

Monyohe could not reply to that. Then Senkepeng ran after her sisters to the mountains, laughing as she went. And as she laughed the mountains and the cliffs laughed with her.

She had hurt him, this girl that he loved. She had hurt him, and he would not be satisfied until he had had revenge on her and all her people. And to do this he took all the water with him when he went back to his father's house that night. He took every drop out of the streams and the pools, so that they were quite dry. *Yo!*

Monyohe had made the sun stand still. He had caused a drought.

The crops withered, they died.

The cattle grew thin, they died.

The clay pots stood empty, for the rivers were dry, and the children cried for food and water.

Their need for water became so great that they had to move to a region where there was water, water so that man and beast could live. But first the big chief, he who was the father of Senkepeng, called his son. His son who answers to the name of Masilo. His father spoke to him:

"Masilo, the drought is bad."

"You speak the truth, father of mine."

"The crops wither, everything is dying."

"It is true, *Morena*."

"The cattle fall down, they die."

"It is so. *Yoalo*."

"The clay pots stand empty, and listen how the children cry for water."

"We all hear it."

"You must seek a place for us where there is water, Masilo."

"Shall we not wait for rain, Father?"

"How can you ask? Do you not know that the young girls have already gone to fetch the porridge stick from the village of Thabaru? And did that bring rain, *ná*?"

"No, *Morena*, it did not bring rain."

"Did the men not kill a lion without any weapons? And did that loosen the rain? I am asking you."

"It did not, Father."

"Did I not myself go in the dark to the clever man to beg for rain? Did I look back once as I walked? No, I did not. I did as I should. I washed my body in a pool of water in the region of the clever man also, before I spoke to him, and did he manage to take away the drought from our land?"

"No, he did not, *Ntate*, father."

"The thirst is choking us all by the throat."

Then Masilo obeyed his father. He took a company of young men with him. He took pack oxen carrying loads of food and water-melons. They took their hunting dogs. Then they walked. They went to search for a place where there was water.

They walked, they walked, they walked, they walked. The dogs ran with them, but wherever they went they only saw dry river beds and dried-up springs. When the thirst nearly strangled them completely they would break open a watermelon and eat the watery flesh almost right to the rind. So they did every day. And when there were no watermelons left, they killed one of the pack oxen. They sucked the water from the contents of the stomach, they ate the meat raw so that the moisture of the blood could take the thirst out of their throats.

They walked farther, farther, farther, and, when they had walked many days, they saw ahead of them spots that shone in the sun. *Mè wheh!*—Mother mine! It was water!

The dogs also saw it and ran toward it. They licked it, they drank it. They swam, they swam, and when they had finished swim-ming they went back to their masters.

"*Mè wheh!* the dogs are wet!" the young men cried.

"*Ghillick*, men, it is water that clings to their hairs!"

Mè wheh, mè wheh, mè wheh!

Then the young men caught the dogs and sucked the moisture out of their fur. They wet their hands on the bodies of the dogs. They rubbed their faces in the damp fur, they pressed their burst lips against it.

Now they had strength again to follow the dogs to the water. When they came to the side of the first pool, they saw with joy that there was much, much water in the pool. The pool was black with the depth of the water. There would be enough water for many people for many moons.

The men fell on the ground and dipped handfuls of water and brought it to their mouths.

Yo na na wheh! Here was a terrible thing! They could not understand it! The water became hard in their hands! It was stone that was touching their lips! They threw the hard stuff away and dipped more water, but it also became hard. Just as before. Just so. *Yoalo.*

They could not find any water to drink, and the thirst would kill them here where they were by the side of so much water! So much water shining in the pool, so much water that was wet in the pool, but that changed to stone as soon as their lips touched it! *Mè wheh!*

Then those big, strong men wept. They wept as a little child weeps when he is very hungry and his mother takes the breast away from his mouth. Just so, just so. *Yoalo.*

Those men wept bitterly, and under the waters Monyohe lay watching them. He heard them weep and he laughed, he laughed, this chief of the waters, just as Senkepeng had laughed at him that day.

Masilo asked, "Who is he that laughs when the thirst has us by the throat?"

And the answer came from the pool like bubbles rising to the surface: "It is Monyohe, owner of the water, it is he."

Now Masilo asked: "If so much water belongs to you, why do you refuse to give us a little handful? We have done you no harm! *Ná*, have we?"

Then Monyohe replied: "It is Senkepeng, the first daughter of your father, who drove the knife into my heart. She laughed at me because I have no arms, I have no legs, because I have no cattle that I can exchange for a bride. That is why I, Monyohe, brought the drought over the people of Senkepeng. That is why. I want to show that young woman how rich you are when you have water."

"If the hand of Senkepeng threw the knife, then only she should be punished, *Morena* Monyohe, and not all of us," argued Masilo.

But the bubbles rising to the surface said: "Give only Senkepeng to me. I have no cattle, *chè*, but I will barter her from you, her big brother, with water."

With a voice nearly dead of drought, Masilo agreed, and he gave his sister to Monyohe as wife. Then the chief loosened the water so that Masilo and his friends could drink.

He also loosened the water where Senkepeng lived. And the water flowed back into the rivers. He loosened the water, and it fell from the sky again, it bubbled up from the springs again.

The crops got water, they grew.

The cattle flourished, they increased.

The clay pots in the huts were full of water again, and the stomachs of the people were yellow once more, for they were full of food and full of water.

But before Masilo went back to his home Monyohe struck a bargain with him. He said: "Big brother of Senkepeng, you need not bring my wife to me. I myself will fetch her. The day that you see a dust cloud rising in the sky, like the smoke from a very big fire, you will know it is Monyohe with his blanket of dust, coming to fetch Senkepeng."

Then a great fear came to the heart of Masilo. His father would not allow his most beloved daughter to go to the *lapa*, the court, of such a creature! He was afraid of the wrath of his father when he heard of the bargain between Masilo and the snake. He remained silent before Monyohe, but on the way back he spoke to the other men. He asked: "*Ná*, did you hear what I promised Monyohe?"

"We did hear, Masilo," they replied.

"My father could kill me."

"*Chè*, it is possible."

"We who know about it must not bite the ears of a single person with that secret. We must sit, sit, sit on the hole of the snake."

"You speak with wisdom, Masilo. Maybe Monyohe does not ever come to fetch Senkepeng."

And they kept their word. Not the great chief, not Senkepeng, nor anyone knew of the price that was paid for the plentiful supply of water they now had.

Only Masilo and his men knew, and they were afraid of the dust cloud that had to come. But they remained quiet. *Tu-u-u-u* . . .

The moons came, the moons grew, the moons died, but Monyohe stayed away. The hearts of those who waited for him went to lie down. The fear went to sleep.

And then the day came that the big snake came to fetch his wife. Wrapped in his blanket of dust, just as he had said, he came over the veld on the tip of his tail, his head high in the air, much higher than the highest tree.

And when Masilo saw it, fear made a coward out of him: a dog that pinches his tail between his legs. He was gray as the ashes of a cold fire when he opened the matter to his sister.

She said nothing. She sat quite still. *Tu-u-u-u* . . .

Then he asked: "Senkepeng, then are you satisfied?"

But she replied that she was not satisfied. How could she be satisfied? How could she?

"What are you going to do, child of my house?" he asked.

And she replied: "The owner of much water is a mighty chief, a great witch doctor. But it is not Senkepeng who will go and sit by him. I shall run, and if that water creature can catch me I shall accept him."

She did not wait but began to run immediately, and, when Monyohe came there and curled himself up in the hut of the great chief, Senkepeng was already behind the first of the red mountains.

The whole tribe knew of the arrival of Monyohe. They streamed to the *lapa*, the court of the chief, and they shuddered when they saw the big *noa*, the big snake lying there. They shuddered when they heard him speak, when they and the father and the mother of Senkepeng heard what his mission was!

It was an upsetting business! The old men of the tribe had to be called together. Blow the horn! In the *khotla*, the gathering of the men of the tribe, it would be decided what to do. Masilo tackled the affair with uncombed hair. Where is she? Where is Senkepeng?

Chè, here is Masilo, but Senkepeng is not here!

"Where is Senkepeng, where is she?"

"She has run away," said Masilo.

And when the people heard this, the whole tribe wailed aloud, because they were afraid that Monyohe would take his water away again and that there would be another long drought.

Masilo went to beg of Monyohe. "*Morena* who is great," said he, "do not punish the whole tribe for a second time when only one is guilty. Senkepeng ran away, and that is right. But she is your wife. If you can catch her, she will go with you. Because you took out water for her, and she sees now that water is greater wealth than cattle."

The whole tribe agreed, for when there is no water the cattle will all die. The man who possesses water is richer than a man who possesses cattle. It is so. *Yoalo*.

Monyohe also was satisfied. "The decision of Senkepeng brings honor to her," he said, "for it becomes a bride to be unwilling and hesitant to meet her bridegroom. It is according to the custom of our ancestors for the girl to run away and for the man to bring her back."

Yo, and then a terrible thing happened! Monyohe uncoiled himself. He uncoiled. He uncoiled. This bridegroom stood on his tail, with his head high, much higher than the highest tree. Now he was going to chase after Senkepeng, and when he disappeared over the first hill they saw that he had already hung his blanket of red dust round his shoulders. Senkepeng also saw the dust coming after her. She was already very tired, but she ran more swiftly than the rabbit does when the dog runs after him. She ran round the mountains, she ran over the muddy bogs, over the veld, but Monyohe came nearer, nearer, nearer.

When she ran by an old shepherd, he saw that Monyohe would overtake her, and he called to her, "Break your necklace of beads!"

She did so and kept running but let the red beads fall on the road. When Monyohe reached that spot, he saw that red ornament of his beloved lying broken in the dust. No, he simply had to pick it up. He picked it up, and, when he had picked up every one of the red beads from the dust, Senkepeng was far ahead again. So far ahead that he could not see her any more.

But he was rested again, and he followed in her footsteps even faster than before. The dust came nearer and nearer to the fleeing Senkepeng, and when she ran by a group of young boys one said to her: "Girl who is beautiful, sing to your pursuer. Sing to him so that he should dance!"

She did so. She sang a very lively song, and the boys sang with her. They clapped their hands as they sang, and when the big snake heard it he began to dance. They sang, he danced. They sang, he danced.

And all the time he was dancing he was knotting, knotting, knotting his long shining body in tight knots. Just so. *Yoalo. Yoalo.*

They kept on singing and he kept on tying tight knots in his body. And when his body was all knotted up and he could not move at all, only then Senkepeng stopped singing and began to run again.

She ran until she came to a village. She was so tired that she could go no farther. The people were astonished to see the beautiful girl who was so tired.

They asked: "*Ná*, why do you run so?"

She told them the whole story. Then they also saw the dust cloud rising behind the mountain and knew that Monyohe had managed to untie the knots.

They made a plan to help the girl: they planted sharp knives in his path, planted them so that only the cutting edges showed above the ground. They did this, and then they waited. They knew that the snake would grow tired. Then he would have to slide on his stomach—on those sharp blades!

And so it happpened. Just so. *Yoalo.*

When Monyohe was very tired, he lay down on his stomach and the red dust settled on him as a skin blanket that is spread over one that sleeps. But Monyohe was not asleep, he was still sliding forward, and that red blanket of dust moved with him. Nearer. Nearer.

And then he came to those sharp knives. And then those who watched saw that red blanket of dust stop. It stopped moving forward. The people did not know what had happened, so they waited. They waited until that red blanket of dust had completely settled on the ground and did not cover Monyohe any more. And then they cautiously went closer to see. And when they reached him they saw that the skin of his stomach was cut open from the tip of his nose to the tip of his tail. And then they saw that the skin was bursting open along that cut. It burst open, but it was not a dead snake that they saw. No, it was a live man who came out of that snakeskin.

Yo, but he was beautiful! He was young and he was strong. Round his shoulders hung a blanket of iron. His hip cloth was also of iron. His shield also. Among all the men gathered there, there was not one better than he. See *thlo*, his stick was the horn of the big rhinoceros! The man shone, he shone, he shone! So beautiful was he!

Everyone could see at once that this Monyohe must be the son of a chief—a man who had been wrapped in the scales of the snake of the deep waters until that very day.

When Senkepeng beheld him, she covered her face with her blanket, for she loved him at once. She loved this man who had exchanged her for water after a long drought, who ran and overtook her when she ran away, as it becomes a betrothed man.

And when they walked back to the village of the father of Senkepeng, the young man walked ahead, as it should be, for he had to protect her. And the young woman walked behind him, as it becomes a woman.

He in front, she behind. Just so. *Yoalo.*

They walked along the road that the feet of their ancestors trod. And so we come to the end of this tale.

Ke tsomo ka mathetho, which means, this is a true tale of the Basotho people.

10. Maliane and the Water Snake

The old people tell other stories of Monyohe also. And one of these is the story of Maliane, the daughter of a chief. She was proud and presumptuous, but her father had a great love for her. She could always do as she pleased, she always had her own way.

She never ate with the other people out of the communal dish, but always received her food separately. She never did any work, other people had to wait on her, and, when she was rude and impertinent, her father only laughed.

But one day she used such ugly language to her mother that her father punished her. It made her very angry. She ran out of the hut and went to sit in the veld. Her little dog, who had followed her, came to sit at her feet. He sat there and looked into her eyes.

"I won't go back to them again," she said to the little dog. "I won't! I won't! I am going to run away!"

"If you run away, Mother," said he, "I will go with you."

So the two ran away. They ran and they ran, and the little dog ran ahead of Maliane to show her the way. They ran until they came to a place where a big thicket of reeds barred the way.

Then the dog spoke. "Mother, you are the daughter of a chief, but even so you have to listen to good advice. It is not good to be rude and impertinent. It is not good at all. If you meet a stranger, talk nicely to him. Do you hear me, Maliane?"

"I hear you," she replied. And just as she finished speaking, a rat peeped out from between the reeds.

"Daughter of a chief, do you want a pathway through the reeds?" he asked.

"Yes, my Big One. Please, Chief," she replied, and the heart of the rat was white for this beautiful and polite girl child. He gnawed down one reed after the other until there was a path through the thicket.

Maliane walked through the reeds, and her little dog followed in her footsteps. Just as they reached the other side, the little dog said to her: "Mother, you did well, and you must continue like that. If we meet strangers you must forget that you are the daughter of a chief. You must forget it completely. Do you hear me, Maliane?"

"Yes, I hear you," she replied. Then they walked farther. They walked, and they walked, and then they saw an old woman sitting by the side of the road. She was very old, and she was very sick. Her whole body was covered by a rash that itched.

"My girl, please scratch my body!" she pleaded. "Please!"

Maliane shuddered at the idea of touching such a sick body, but she remembered the advice that the little dog had given her. She scratched, she scratched, she scratched until the old one's skin itched no longer.

"Your heart is good," said the old woman. "Now I will also make it strong for you." She made two rows of cuts across the breast of Maliane. It looked like two strings of beads hanging round her neck. In the cuts she rubbed powerful medicine that was mixed with soot. And when she had finished, she had finished.

Maliane thanked the old woman. Then she walked farther, and in her footsteps the little dog followed.

"You did well, Mother," said he. "One person must always help another. There comes a time that you need help yourself, and then the other one will help you."

They walked, they walked, they walked. They came to a fountain. When Maliane was about to drink, she saw a crippled woman standing beside her clay pot. The crippled woman said to her: "My sister, you are young and fresh. Help me to put the clay pot on my head."

Maliane first wanted to say that she was the daughter of a chief and could not wait on others, for she was the one to be waited on. But once more she thought of the advice of her little dog, and she helped the poor woman with the clay pot.

"You have helped me, young woman," said she who was crippled. "Now I want to help you too. Do you see the blue smoke hanging in the air beside the mountain? It comes from the fires that burn in the cooking shelters of the chief of this region. He has a son who will be chief after him, and he has not yet got a wife. If you follow my advice, you will be the woman for whom this great man will chase cattle from his herd. You are kind, your heart is strong, and you are beautiful, as the wife of a chief should be."

"What does the young man look like?" asked Maliane.

"*Yo*, we don't know. They keep him in the hut all the time, such is the care they take of him. There is not one person who has seen him. But his mother says he is very strong and very brave. They have not yet seen a girl who is good enough for him."

"Will I be good enough?" asked Maliane.

"You will be good enough if you follow my advice."

"What is your advice, Big Woman?"

"You must go, go, go to the chief's house. You must go and stand by the door of the screen in front of his house. You must wait, wait, wait until someone sees you. And, if they ask you what you seek, you must say that I sent you to them. Then they will ask you to come in. If you behave well, you will certainly become the wife of their son."

"How must I behave?" asked Maliane.

"You must never take bread before the others. Let the others take bread and eat first. If they give you a new gourd to drink from, you must say that an old one is good enough for you. Always you must do thus. *Yoalo, yoalo!*"

Maliane did so. When she told the wife of the chief that she was the daughter of another chief, they treated her very nicely. When they spread open a skin for her to sit on, she said that the bare ground was best for her. When they gave her a new stone to grind corn on, she said she preferred an old one. When they went to fetch water, she gave the other women the new clay pot and took the cracked one herself.

"Hm!" said the wife of the chief after they had left with the clay pots. "She is beautiful, that Maliane. And she is not proud. She is not presumptuous. She is the woman for our son."

That evening the old woman took Maliane to the hut of her son. When the fire built by the serving girls began to light up the room, she saw much food: cooked meat and offal together with the intestines, corn cakes, leaf stew, curds, and beer. *Yo!* It was food for many people!

"Who eats all this food?" asked Maliane.

"Your bridegroom," replied the wife of the chief. "He eats it all."

"When does he come?" asked Maliane.

"As soon as the fire has burned down, when it is dark in the hut."

Then the old woman went away and Maliane waited alone for her bridegroom. She wondered about the terrible man who could eat so much food all by himself. She wondered, she wondered. When she became sleepy, she unrolled her sleeping mat and lay down on it to sleep. She called her little dog to come and lie beside her, but he did not want to do so. He ran to and fro in the hut, he smelled the ground, he smelled the walls, then he whined softly for a while, softly, so that the others could not hear him, only Maliane. She thought he wanted to eat some of the food, so she opened the door and chased him out.

She sprinkled water on the fire to quench it, and when it was dark she went to lie down again on the sleeping mat.

In the dark she heard something stir in the room. It breathed. It brushed against the reed thatch of the roof. It came down to the ground. Maliane heard it devour the meat, eat the other food, slurp up the beer.

"It must be my husband," said the heart of Maliane, "but I cannot see him." She wondered what kind of a man it would be who lay on the top of the wall, beneath the roof, and waited for the dark. She wondered. She wondered.

When he had eaten all the food, he groaned aloud and said: "Monyohe has found a wife. She lies on the sleeping mat. Monyohe is now going to sleep beside his wife."

Maliane was afraid, for she knew that Monyohe was the great snake of the deep waters. But the old woman had made her heart strong, so she did not cry out at all. She lay quite still.

Tu-u-u-u . . .

Monyohe slithered to her sleeping mat, he curled his long, slippery body in a coil beside his wife and laid his head on her breast. Then he slept, but Maliane lay awake until she heard the cocks begin to weep. Then she slept. When she awoke, her bridegroom had gone. There he lay again on the top of the wall, in the opening between the ceiling and the wall, and he looked down at her with his little beady eyes.

"I am going to fetch water for you, Big Man," said Maliane.

Then she took the clay pot and walked swiftly to the spring, and her little dog trotted after her. But when she came to the water she threw away the clay pot and fled from that place. She did not look back, she just ran. Later she heard somebody breathing behind her:

ffoo, ffoo, ffoo! and she knew that it was her husband following her. When the little dog wanted to attack him, he lashed out at the dog with his tail, and when he reached Maliane he beat her with the tail as a real man beats his wife with his stick.

She ran and he followed her.

She ran and he beat her with his tail.

When she reached the hut of her parents she was so tired that she fell down on the floor inside the hut. They picked her up and gave her water to drink. The little dog called all the dogs together, and they attacked the snake. He fled and went to hide by the spring.

"I want more water," said Maliane. "The thirst is choking me."

But there was no more water in the house. Maliane's mother ran down to the spring to go and dip water, but when she came there she saw the big snake lying in the water, and she was too afraid to go nearer.

Yo wheh! What a fright! Where was the witch doctor? He had to be called. He must come and kill the snake. They called the witch doctor, he came. But when he saw the snake he knew it was Monyohe, the son of a chief, and he remembered wrapping Monyohe in the skin of the water snake when he was a baby.

"Kill an ox for us," he commanded.

They killed the ox.

"Make a fire by the mouth of the spring."

They made a fire.

"Give me a piece of the ox fat!"

They brought it.

The witch doctor threw the fat on the glowing embers, and the smoke filled the cave around the spring. Monyohe smelled it. He came out of the water. *Yo,* then the people ran away, they were so afraid of that terrible creature. But when they turned round they saw a wonderful thing: as a snake climbs out of his old skin when he sheds it, so Monyohe climbed out of the skin of the water snake. But it was not a snake that climbed out, it was a man! Round his shoulders hung a blanket of jackal skin, in his hand he held a spear and a skin shield. He had become a young man with a strong body and fiery eyes. He spoke like one who was a chief already.

"Where is Maliane?" he said authoritatively. "Make way before me, I want to go to my wife!"

The people were so frightened that they could not talk, and, when Monyohe came to his wife, she immediately loved him with a love that was red.

Monyohe's father gave a whole corral full of cattle as bride price for Maliane. And after the big wedding feast she went with her husband to his house, and here the story comes to an end.

Ke tsomo ka mathetho, which means: this is a true tale of the Basotho people.

11. Molaetsane

They still tell the story of Molaetsane. She was a young heifer. Reddish yellow she was, and she belonged to Bulane. He was a great chief, who owned much cattle. But of all the cattle he loved Molaetsane best, he had loved her best ever since she was a tiny calf.

Chè, he loved her a lot. And when he called her she broke away from the herd and came to him. That was how much she loved him too. She loved him as if he were her father.

But as time went by, they saw that there was something wrong with Molaetsane. The other young heifers who were born in the same year were all feeding on the mountainside with their own firstborn calves, but the reddish yellow one still had no calf.

"*Yo!*" said the old men, "there is something very wrong with Molaetsane of Bulane."

"She is a danger to our herds," said another. "She must be killed," said a third. "It is against the tradition of our ancestors that she should live."

They went to talk to the chief. They opened their hearts to him.

Molaetsane is not a cow that may be allowed to live, she had to be killed, they said.

"*Chè!*" cried Bulane. "I will not give my permission in this matter. Molaetsane must not be killed!"

But she must not stay among the other cows, said they. They were aware that Bulane was their great chief, but the old men wanted to remind him that a rotten tooth will also cause its neighbor to ache.

No, it was the truth they spoke, but he asked them for time to think about this matter. You cannot grab a termite by its head while it is still emerging from the hole—you must bide your time.

Bulane thought it over, and then he realized that there was only one way open to him. Only one way. Then he let the old ones gather and told them how his heart had spoken to him: he would send Molaetsane away, far away, so that she could do no harm to the cows that stayed behind.

The old ones were satisfied. Bulane had decided to do the right thing. Then their hearts went to lie down. *Tu-u-u.*

The heart of Bulane was altogether black. But he had promised, and he could not swallow his words.

He sent Molaetsane away. The men who took her away did not only walk one day long: it was three days that they walked. Then they came to a place like the one that Bulane had told them to find.

There was much water. There was shelter, and the grass grew thick and tall. It was a place where Molaetsane would want for nothing.

But when the men went back to the region of Bulane, the eyes of the reddish yellow heifer followed them sorrowfully. She lowed sadly after them, but they shut their ears and walked quickly away from the lonely one.

When the dark came, Molaetsane went to sleep, and when the day broke she began to dig stones from the side of the mountain. She dug with her horns. She dug with her hoofs. She gathered the stones. And when she had enough she built a corral for cattle. And when the corral was finished, her unfruitfulness was taken away from her and she began to calve. She calved full-grown cattle and calves also. Many, many times, until there was room for no more in the corral.

And then she built a second one. And when it was finished she filled it with sheep that she gave birth to—she who had been un-fruitful.

Now she was a rich woman, that reddish yellow cow. She was the mother of many. But she had not yet finished. She built huts. Many huts, until they formed a village. She built a wall around it, and when all was finished she became the mother of animals again. But this time it was goats. Many goats until all the huts were full. Rams and ewes.

Au, and then that great woman Molaetsane was very happy. The ewes worked for her: they were her children. They worked for the reddish yellow one who was their mother and their mistress. They ground corn for her, they brewed beer for her. It was the ewes that saw to it that Molaetsane did not go hungry. It was the ewes who made porridge for her. They went to fetch water for her from the springs, carrying it in clay pots that they made themselves from clay that they dug out of the river bank. The ewes carried the pots on their heads, for they walked on their hind legs just like the women of humans do. And the ewes also cooked the meat for their mother, meat that the rams brought home from the hunt. The rams provided well for the cow that was their mistress and their mother.

And, as was the way with men, the billy goats lay in the sun and slept when it was cold and smoked marijuana when they woke up. They drank the beer that the women brought to them in clay pots.

No, they lived well, those goats, the rams and the ewes. And Molaetsane had no complaints at the *khotlas*, the gatherings of the people.

And then she calved once more. It was not an animal, it was a human: a boy child.

Molaetsane, the reddish yellow cow, put her son down on the corral wall and washed him with her tongue. And when she had licked him clean, she hung a *karos,* a skin blanket, round his little shoulders.

She gave him a shield made of skin.

She gave him a spear. And she gave him a hunting knife. Just so. *Yoalo.*

She fed him milk.

That boy child of the cow drank the milk. He drank the milk, he drank the milk, he grew and he grew. He was very beautiful, that young man, and he was strong, but he never saw any other humans. He only knew the animals, and he loved his mother, the cow, very much.

She talked with him. She told him of other humans, of her master Bulane, who did not want to have her killed when she deserved to be killed. Now he wished that he too could see what other humans looked like. Then the cow made a plan.

She let the sun stand still, so that a great drought came to the land of Bulane. The drought brought famine with it, and, when the stomachs of the people were cold because there was no food and the thirst choked their throats, then Bulane thought of the fruitful place where they had taken the reddish yellow cow. Then he sent a few young men to go and see what the land looked like there, whether there was water, whether there was food.

When the young men came to the village of the reddish yellow cow, they saw a number of men talking. It was a gathering of goats, but they spoke like men. They said: "We greet you, travelers! Where do you come from?"

"We come from the land of Bulane. We seek food and water and grazing for our cattle. Where we come from there is a great drought. There is hunger."

"*Hê?*" cried the goats.

"Yes," replied the young men. Then the goats told the news to their mother, the cow. She was very glad that her plan had worked so well. She called her son to come and see what people looked like. Everybody was glad about the humans. The ewes carried food to the visitors on their heads: porridge and meat and beer. The joy was great. When it was evening and everyone had a full stomach, the visitors and the goats and the young man who was the son of the cow all danced around the fires.

Then they slept.

When the dark became light the following morning, the visitors had to return to Bulane, who had sent them. The ewes prepared food for the journey. They filled the visitors' gourds with water, but before they left the cow told them to let Bulane know that there was enough room for all his people and all their cattle and that he should bring every one to that place where the reddish yellow cow and her people lived.

When the men brought the greetings of the reddish yellow cow to Bulane, his heart was altogether white. He was very glad that the cow still lived and that things had gone well for her.

They did not wait. Bulane called the headmen together and told them to command the people to pack all their belongings and gather their cattle together, so that they could trek to the land of the reddish yellow cow.

They did so, and when they came to that land they were amazed to see how much had been built: how beautiful the village and the corrals of the cow were. They were astonished to see how rich she was, and they were dumbfounded when they saw her child, he who was a man already. They could only keep on saying, "*Aaaaa! Aaaaaa!*"

Every heart was glad. Bulane and his people were now in a land where food and water were plentiful, and, when their stomachs were warm from all the food they ate that night, they began to dance and sing. They danced and sang right through that night until the darkness became light. And that day Molaetsane divided her land in two great parts, one part for herself and her son, and the other part for Bulane and his people.

She divided the grazing. She divided the streams and she divided the food. The one half for herself and the other half for Bulane. Just so. *Yoalo. Yoalo.*

And when she had finished, she had finished.

They live in peace.

And this is the end of the story.

12. Obe, the Monster of the Dark Canyon

The old people tell of a young girl who married a man who came from a far-off place. She did not know his people, and she did not know of the deeds of his people, deeds that were done in the dark.

And after she was married she worked for her mother-in-law, as it should be. She winnowed the corn, she ground the wheat, she brewed the beer, she strained it . . . she worked the whole day long. At night, when she had finished working, she went to sleep. But the next day when she rose she would see that all the food she had prepared the day before was gone. The clay pots were empty!

Ghillick! It was an ugly thing that took place in the dark of the night!

The next day she winnowed corn again, she ground it, she made porridge. And when she had cooked the porridge she formed balls of it in her hands. So she made corn balls. She put them down on the grass mat to dry. When evening came, she put them away carefully in the hut, so that the hungry dogs should not eat them during the night. But, when the dark grew light the next day, there were no more corn balls on the grass mat . . . they had disappeared as the other food and the beer had disappeared.

She thought: *Ghillick!* In the dark things happened that she could not understand, here among the tribe into which she had married. But she kept silent. She told no one.

The next day she cooked meat. She rendered the fat down and put it in the hut with the rest of the meat, so that the cats should not eat it when the light became dark. When she had finished, she went to sleep. But when all the other people were asleep also, something came to wake this young woman. It was the mother of her husband.

She talked to the young woman: "Wife of my son, rise so that we can take food to my people."

And the young woman asked: "Who are your people? And why must we take food to them in the middle of the night?"

Then the mother-in-law replied: "Hang your skin blanket round your shoulders and put the cooked meat and the fat on your head. I will show you the way to my people."

Her daughter obeyed her, for had that big woman not taken cattle and sheep out of her herds to pay for her? So she carried the clay pot on her head and followed the big woman into the night.

They walked, they walked, they walked, they walked. They came to a very deep canyon. It was a very deep canyon with many trees and bushes growing in it. It was quiet. It was dark.

But the big woman walked deeper and deeper into the canyon, through the trees. Then they heard the snoring of many people asleep: *hò-na, hò-na, hò-na!* The young woman became very frightened, but her mother-in-law walked on until they reached the sleeping ones.

It was frightening!

There were baboons, there were spirits, there were other wild animals and ghosts that no one had ever seen before. They sat hunched up. They slept. They snored. Then the young woman knew that the mother of her husband was practicing witchcraft in this dark canyon. And she was afraid there in that dark canyon with her mother-in-law and all the sleeping creatures.

But her mother-in-law said: "Do not be afraid, my child. I am going to teach the secrets of witchcraft to you also. Do you see these two whips?"

"I see, *Mè*."

"Here is the whip that is black, and here is the whip that is brown."

"I see, *Mè*."

Then the big woman took the black whip and threatened the sleeping ones with it. She threatened them, and they all died. They snored no more. They were quite dead.

She asked: "Do you see what happens when I threaten my people with the black whip?"

"I see, *Mè*."

Then the big woman took the whip that was brown and she threatened the dead ones with it. Then they woke again. They were alive.

"Do you see what happens when I threaten them with a whip that is brown?"

"I see, *Mè*."

Then the big woman gave her the two whips in her hands. She said: "Threaten us now with the whips so that I can see whether you understand."

She took the black whip. She threatened the people with it, just as her mother-in-law had done. And when she did so, they all died. At once.

But she did not wake them again with the brown whip. She left them lying there dead in the dark, and she ran away, away out of that canyon. She went back to the house of her own people, her own father and mother.

They were very surprised when they saw her. They said to her: "What are you doing here?"

And she replied: "You gave me to a woman who is a witch. She wants to teach me also, but I am too afraid, for it is something that takes place in the dark."

Her parents understood this and allowed her to live with them again.

Now: about those "people" in the canyon. They woke up when the sun rose. The ghosts disappeared and the other weird creatures could be seen no longer. And the big woman went back to her home. She was very angry at the wife of her son. She thought she would find her at home, but she was not there. She searched for her daughter-in-law, but when she saw that she was gone she knew that the young woman had gone back to the house of her parents.

But she could do nothing. She had to wait until it became dark again. Then she went back to the canyon. She heard her people snoring, *hò-na, hò-na, hò-na,* and she woke them up with the whip that was brown. When they were sleeping no longer, she called Obe.

Now, this Obe was a dreadful creature. He was the biggest of them all in the canyon. He was the strongest. His ears were as big as a human being. He was a frightening creature, but when he sang it was so beautiful that no one could hear it and stay awake. Everyone fell asleep.

Now the big woman sent Obe. She said: "Go and fetch the wife of my son. She belongs to my house, because I exchanged her for much cattle."

Obe went.

When he reached the entrance of the village where the young woman was, he started to sing. He sang so beautifully and his song was so sweet that all the people in the village fell asleep immediately, like small children when their mothers sing them to sleep. He sang this song:

Obe! Obe! Obe!
What do you say, what do you see, Obe?
Daughter of men, Obe,
Ears standing up, Obe.

Only the young woman stayed awake. She heard the song of Obe, and she was afraid when she saw her parents fall asleep and when she heard them snore *hò-na, hò-na, hò-na.*

"Father!" she called. "Mother!" They did not hear her. "Wake up!" she called. "Do you not hear the danger that threatens, the danger that is coming closer?"

But her father slept. He snored. And her mother slept. She snored.

Then she ran to the hut that stood next to theirs.

"You, man!" she called. "You, man, do you not know of the danger that threatens, the danger that is coming closer?"

But the man slept. The woman slept. They both snored.

Then she ran back to her own house. She wept, for the song was very near now:

Obe! Obe! Obe!
What do you say, what do you see, Obe?
Daughter of men, Obe,
Ears standing up, Obe.

She wept with fear, she crawled inside her blankets and pulled them above her head and sat very still. *Tu-u-u* . . .

But Obe was a creature with magic powers, and he came straight to the house of her parents. He came in, he picked her up and put her inside his ear and carried her away, back to the canyon where the mother-in-law and the ghosts and the baboons and the other creatures waited for her in the dark.

When Obe came there the big woman told all her subjects that they must go among the bushes and trees and pick switches that they can use as whips. They did so, and when they came back they whipped the young woman with these whips. They whipped her, they whipped her, they whipped her. Then the mother-in-law commanded Obe to take her back to her parents.

The next night when it was dark, everything happened in the same way again. Just so. *Yoalo.* When Obe came to get the young woman he sang so sweetly—Obe! Obe! Obe!—that everyone fell asleep, that everyone snored. Only she whom he came to fetch stayed awake, and she heard him come. Nearer. Nearer. Nearer.

She heard the soothing song—Obe! Obe! Obe!—louder, louder, louder. And when he picked her up he put her inside his ear to carry her to the canyon where they whipped her. Then the creature would take her back to her parents.

The next day the same again. *Yoalo.*

And the day after the same again. *Yoalo.*

Then her father went to find a clever witch doctor. He took much cattle from his herds, so that the feet of the clever man could walk to his village. And when he had paid him with that cattle, the man said *chè*, now his feet could go.

And, when he came to that woman who had been whipped, the witch doctor said that the father must first take a sheep out of his herd. The sheep would open the little bag in which all the magic bones and the magic stones slept. And when he had the sheep he said *chè*, now the bag could open.

Then the clever man threw the bones and the stones on the ground, but they would not talk. They refused to speak, they refused. Then the father took out another sheep. *Chè*, then those bones spoke.

Ghillick! Those bones spoke with wisdom! And the people obeyed the commands of the magic bones of that clever man.

When it became night, they divided the old men, the young men, and the warriors into groups. On this side of the road one group hid themselves. On the other side of the road another group hid themselves. All along the sides of the road groups of men hid themselves.

Just so. In the shelter behind the reed screen in front of the hut another group of men hid themselves. On either side of the door a few stood guard, and the others sat inside the hut.

They waited.

They waited for Obe.

When the creature with the big ears came, they heard his singing. He sang so sweetly! All the people heard it, but they did not fall asleep, for the clever witch doctor had given them medicine to keep the sleep away from their eyes.

Now everyone sat there wide awake. They heard the song of Obe. It grew louder, louder, louder. Obe! Obe! Obe! They heard the song. It was soothing, like the song children sing when they want to sing baby chickens to sleep. Obe! Obe! Obe!

It was then that the creature with the ears arrived at the hut of the young woman. He went inside the reed screen in front of the hut, he wanted to enter by the door of the hut. But he did not go inside, for it was then that the men came out from behind the hut with their spears and their clubs and killed him with their spears and their clubs.

They killed him.

He died.

He, Obe.

But when the mother-in-law there in the canyon saw that Obe was not returning, she went to look for him. She walked, she walked, she walked, and when the sun began to shine she came to the hut of her daughter-in-law and saw the creature with the big ears lying there on the ground.

Oe na! Oh me! It was a big loss, and then she knew that the power of the witch doctor was greater than her own power. She threatened Obe with the whip that was brown, but he stayed dead.

Then she asked them for the skin of Obe, but they did not want to give it to her. They knew that with the skin of Obe she would make bad medicine that would cause a great deal of evil in the dark. And so she went back to her house.

But the people spoke much about this woman and her bad deeds. They told, told, told it to each other until it reached the ears of the chief. When he heard that the woman was a witch he chased her out of his region. They set the dogs on her and she ran until they could see her no more.

And so the story finds its end.

Ke tsomo ka mathetho, which means, this is a true tale of the Basotho people.

13. The Dove, the Heron, and Jackal

They tell of the story of Leeba, the dove, and her three children, the *leebana*. Their nest was in the branches of a big willow tree. The willow tree grew in a marsh, where grass and flowers grew in the watery soil.

Kokolofito, the heron, the man with the long legs and the long neck, came every day to hunt in the little pools for frogs and other small animals that live in the water. Leeba, the dove, was his friend. He loved her very much. He loved her children very much also. The little *leebana* who always talked so nicely to each other, *cheep-cheep, cheep-cheep, cheep-cheep!*

No, the heart of Kokolofito was white for Leeba and the three little *leebana*.

But one day Jackal came to the marsh. He was looking for food. He heard how nicely the little doves were talking to each other, *cheep-cheep*, high up in the willow tree. That is food, he said to himself. Tender meat!

But the nest was high, and the nest was among the branches of the willow tree, and the mother of Jackal had never taught him how to climb trees. But he was a clever man, and he made his voice thick.

He made his voice thick, and he called to the mother of the *lee-bana*: "Throw one of your little ones down to me, or I'll climb up the tree and eat you all!"

Yo, what could she do? She did as he said. She threw one child down to him. He ate it up. Altogether. The feathers also.

"That tasted good," he called. "Tomorrow I'll come and get another, Leeba!" And he left.

But Leeba, she remained sitting on her nest and she wept over her child.

She wept, she wept, she wept over the *leebana*.

Kokolofito heard his friend weeping—"*Oo-oo-oo-oo!*"

He asked her why it was that she mourned so. She told him. She told him of Jackal who had eaten her child. With feathers and all. Everything!

"Tomorrow he will come and fetch the second one. *Oo-oo-oo-oo!*" Her heart would not lie down.

"*Au*, my friend, you were stupid," said Kokolofito and swung his long neck to and fro, to and fro. "You must not throw your child down to Phokoyo! He cannot climb trees! He cannot! His mother never showed him how to!"

"What are you saying?" asked Leeba. She was amazed.

"If he comes again you must laugh at him when he says that he will climb the tree to eat you up. He cannot do it. Do you hear me?"

"I hear you, Grandfather. I shall do as you say."

The next day Phokoyo, the Jackal, came to the tree again.

"Throw one of your children down to me," he growled with his thick voice, "or I'll climb up there and eat you all up!"

But Leeba did not do as he said. Instead, she laughed at him. "Your words are like milk in a sieve. You cannot climb a tree at all. Your mother never showed you how to!"

Jackal was dumbfounded.

"Where do you come by this wisdom?" Phokoyo was angry, for he was hungry.

"Kokolofito told me."

"That bird! With his ugly long neck! Where is that fellow?"

"There he stands among the reeds."

Phokoyo walked to him. He came to the heron, but that man did not look up. He stood on one leg and looked in the water. He did not look up at all. *O-yo-yo-yo!*

"Kokolofito!" cried Jackal. "When the wind comes from that direction, over there, where will you look?"

Heron asked, "You! Where will you look, Phokoyo?"

Jackal replied, "I will look in this direction."

Then Kokolofito said: "Me too. Then I will also look in this same direction."

Then Jackal asked: "Kokolofito, *ná*, where will you look when the rain falls to that side over there? *Ná?*"

Kokolofito replied, "You! Which way will you look?"

"I shall look away," replied Phokoyo, "in that direction."

"Me too," said Kokolofito. "I shall look in the same direction as you."

Then Phokoyo asked: "And if the rain falls down straight from above? Which way will you look then, Kokolofito?"

"*Ná*, which way will you look, Jackal?"

"I shall hold my hands over my head. Like this! Do you see?"

"That is what I shall do also, Phokoyo," said Kokolofito, and he spread his wings. He folded them over his head so that they covered his head altogether.

And when his eyes were covered by his wings Phokoyo grabbed him by his long neck. "Now I am going to eat you up, for it was you who told Leeba of my plan. And it is because of you that I am going around with a stomach that is cold from hunger."

He tightened his grip on Heron's throat. Kokolofito was afraid that Jackal might strangle him altogether.

"My friend," he said, "I am very sorry that I told Leeba about you. Let me go. I beg you. Just let go a little so that my voice can come through. Then I can tell you where there is plenty of food. I know where Sheep has lambed. She now has ten children."

Kokolofito was speaking so softly, so softly, that Jackal could hardly hear what he was saying. But this was a matter that he wanted to know more about. Where Sheep and her ten children lived. That would be better food than the flesh of Kokolofito would be!

Jackal took his hands off the neck of Kokolofito, and he asked, he asked nicely: "Tell me, Big Man! Where is Sheep, with those ten lamb children of hers?"

"I cannot speak when my beak is covered," said Kokolofito, and he took his wings away from his head. He shook them, and Jackal sat and waited for him to speak and tell him where Sheep and her ten children were.

Kokolofito spread his wings, and, before he could say a single word about Sheep, he lifted himself from the ground and went to sit in the top of the willow tree. In the top of the willow tree, right beside the nest with Leeba and the little *leebana*, the dove and the two little doves in their nest.

There he was safe. He knew that very well. Phokoyo would never be able to reach him there. He cannot climb a tree at all, for his mother never showed him how to.

Ke tsomo ka mathetho, which means, this is a true tale of the Basotho people.

14. The Mother-in-Law and the Clear Water

The people tell of a woman who was very old. She could not go to the veld with the other women any more to pick up kindling for the fires, because her back had grown too stiff. She could not carry water in clay pots on her head any more, because her neck was already too crooked. She could not go to the fields any more to hoe, for her legs could not carry her so far any more, and her arms did not have the strength any more to swing a hoe. She could not even take care of the children of her children any more, because they ran away from her and laughed at her and mocked her when she could not catch them.

She worked no more, for she had finished working.

So every day she sat in the sweet sunlight, so that her cold body could grow warm. She sat alone, for the men went to the mountains to hunt, the women went to the fields to hoe, and the bigger children carried the little ones on their backs and went to the veld to dig up roots that they could eat and pick the leaves of plants growing by the ash heaps, leaves to cook in stews.

Then the grandmother would sit quite still, in the shelter of the reed screen in front of the hut, until she could hear their voices no longer. And, when she was sure that no one could see her, she would go into the hut of the husband of her daughter. Then she would put on his clothes, hang his *karos*, his skin blanket, round her, take his spoon and his bowl, and then she would sit in his seat and drink the sour milk that was kept in a gourd for him.

And when he came back from the hunt he would see the mother of his wife, sitting by herself in the sweet sunlight. But, when he wanted to drink his sour milk to slake his thirst, he would see that someone had already drunk of it.

Every day, every day the same thing would happen. When he asked his wife and children who it was who took his sour milk, not one of them would know. And the old woman would say nothing. She sat quite still. *Tu-u-u . . .*

The husband then made a plan. He pretended to go to the mountains to hunt, but when he had gone a little way from the hut he turned back and made his way through the bushes to the hut. Nobody had seen him.

Nobody had seen him, and he hid near the hut because he wanted to know who it was who drank his sour milk every day.

When the young women had finished their work they took their hoes and went to the fields, and the children went to the veld to dig up roots and to pick leaves for stew from the plants that grew so thickly by the ash heaps.

When all the people had gone away, when it became quiet in the village, when the old one knew that there was no one to see her, she stood up. She put on the clothes of the man, she hung his blanket round her, she went to sit in his seat, and she began to eat the sour milk from his gourd.

Alaala! How angry that man was! He scolded the old one. He scolded her, he scolded her. And to punish her he sent her to fetch clear water for him. He said: "Bring me water to drink, my throat is dry from thirst and the sour milk is not enough to take away that thirst. Go and fetch me some clear water, but you must dip from a place where there is not a single frog in the water."

She did not argue, for she knew that she had done wrong. She took a small clay pot and she went to the spring. She looked in the dipping place, she looked in the reeds that grew around the spring, but she saw no frog. Then she dipped water with the dipping gourd and filled the clay pot.

But, just as she had finished, she heard "*koo-rooo! koo-rooo!*" It was a frog! She could not see him, but she could hear him crying deep under the water.

She walked, she walked, she walked until she came to the stream. But she did not dip water, because even as she came close to the stream she heard the frogs jump from the banks into the water: *d-duma, d-duma, d-duma.*

She walked farther. Now she went to the mountains. There she would surely find clear water in the little mountain stream.

She climbed until she reached the clear mountain stream. She heard only the sound that water makes when it flows over rocks, she did not hear any frog crying at all. Here she would find clear water. She held her pot under the little waterfall, but just as she had enough she heard from higher up, from the place where the water came from, a frog crying "*koo-rooo! koo-rooo!*"

She could not see him, she could only hear him crying "*koo-rooo! koo-rooo! koo-rooo!*"

When she had thrown away this water also, she walked farther again. It grew dark and she was tried, and she slept just where she was, in the veld, and when the dark grew light again she hunted farther and farther for water.

But at all the springs it was "*koo-rooo! koo-rooo!*"

And at all the pools it was *d-duma, d-duma!*

After she had searched for water for many days, she came to the place where the animals drink. There she heard no frogs jumping in the water, she heard no frogs crying. Then the old one stood on her knees by the water and began to dip from the pool.

The animals saw her—and it was an important matter! Here was an old human being stealing their drinking water! They had never heard of such a thing. They caught the old woman, they caught her and carried her off to the chief of all the animals.

They took her to Lion, for he was the master of the drinking water.

Lion was very angry about the thing that had happened. The humans were the enemies of the animals—they killed animals! And now they even came to make trouble at the drinking pool of the animals! No, this was a thing that had to be punished.

They held court and all the animals were satisfied at the verdict of the chief. He said he would punish the old woman himself the next day.

Then they went to bed. But in the middle of the night Rabbit got up. He went to the old one and woke her.

He said: "*Ko-ko, ko-ko.*" He said, "Get up, Grandmother mine! I want to take you home!" She got up quickly, and they went away quietly.

But it had been raining a lot, and the path was full of mud, but Rabbit helped her until they were nearly at her house. At the ash heaps he turned round.

When he reached the place of the animals again they were still all asleep. He took mud and smeared it on the feet and legs of Rock Hare. When Rock Hare was covered with mud, Rabbit went to a pool and washed all the mud off himself, and then he laid down and went to sleep.

When the animals got up they searched for the old woman, but they could not find her. Then Rabbit said: "Why is all that mud on the body of Rock Hare? Is it not proof that he has been walking in the rain? Why did he walk in the rain? I'll tell you. He took the grandmother back to her people."

"You speak with wisdom," said Lion, and he commanded that Rock Hare be punished. And the animals took Rock Hare and punished him.

And then Rabbit began to boast. He said: "They think it was Rock Hare, but all the time it was I. They thought it was Hlolo, and all the time it was Mutla."

"What are you saying, Rabbit?" asked all the other animals.

But he laughed and said, "I said the wind is blowing in the trees."

But they had heard him very well the first time, and now they knew that he was lying. They were also very tired of Mutla, the rabbit. He did as he pleased and never was punished. But now he had admitted before all of them that he had tricked them.

And now it was their chance to punish him also. They wanted to catch him, but he simply ran away. He ran so quickly that no one could catch him. He fled to the old woman, to her whom he had helped in the night.

When he reached the village all the people were away, as they were every day. *Yoalo.* Just so. But the old one sat alone in the shelter of the reed screen, where the sweet sunlight could reach her, warm her.

Hunger had now caught up with Rabbit, for he had run very far, and, when he saw the grandmother sitting alone like that, he killed her. He threw her in a pot, and he cooked her. He cooked her until she became meat to eat.

Then the men came back from the hunt, and the women came back from the fields, and the children came back from the veld.

They were all hungry. All of them.

But they saw Mutla. He jumped around in the shelter of the reed screen, he dished meat from the pot for everybody, meat that they could eat. His own stomach had been filled long ago. The others ate. They ate.

Then the woman said: "I do not see Grandmother. Where is she?"

And Mutla replied with a lie: "She went to pick up dried dung for the fires."

They believed him and kept on eating the fine meat that he offered them again and again.

But then one of the children shouted: "*Yo wheh!* Here is Grandmother's finger in my meat!"

But Mutla replied: "Not at all! She took her fingers with her when she went to the veld."

Then they again believed Mutla, and they ate all the good meat that he served them. But just as they finished, he began to laugh. He laughed, he laughed, he laughed. Then he said to them: "It is your grandmother that you have eaten. You have eaten her up altogether, her fingers also."

Yo, but they were angry! They tried to catch him, but there is no one who can catch Mutla when he is running his fastest. He ran, but the men with the dogs ran, also, and did not stop. At last Rabbit was so tired that he simply could go no farther, so he quickly cut off his two long ears and went and sat down as innocently as can be, right in the path of his pursuers. He sat in the path, for he knew that no one would recognize him without his ears.

The men saw the animal with its strange raggedy ears, but ran past him, and as soon as they had disappeared over the next hill Mutla darted away and went to the home of Mother Baboon, where she lived with her five children.

He spoke very politely to her. "*Mè*," he said, "aren't you looking for someone to take care of your children in the daytime, while you go and cut grass?"

"I need someone like that," she replied.

"I am the one who could do that for you," he said. Then Mother Baboon was very glad, because now her heart could be at ease when she was working far away from home.

But, Rabbit was not only clever, he was also heartless. Every day he cooked one of the children he had to tend. He cooked one, and, when he had eaten his fill, he would keep some of the meat for his employer, Mother Baboon.

She would eat it, and, when she had eaten enough, she would say to her servant, "Now bring the children so that I can nurse them."

Then Mutla would bring the children that were still alive to the mother, one by one, and when they had finished nursing, he would bring those that had already nursed to the mother again, so that she should still think she had five children who were nursing.

Every day he cooked one. The first day, the second day, the third day, the fourth day.

Now only one child was left. Mutla brought him five times to nurse, but Mother Baboon did not notice that anything was wrong. She was satisfied, for she did not hear her children crying. She did not know that there was only the one child that she was holding to her breast.

And the next day when the big woman, the mother of that last child, went again to cut grass, Mutla killed him also. Then he cooked him too until he became meat and he ate until he had had enough, and that which was left over he gave to Mother Baboon when she returned that afternoon.

When her stomach was full, she said to her servant, "Bring my children, so that they can nurse."

But Rabbit replied, "They are not hungry, they do not want to nurse."

But she was a clever woman, that Mother Baboon. She knew that Mutla was lying to her and that he had cooked her children until they became meat. Her heart was black, and she wanted to avenge the death of her children. She flew at Mutla, but he had always been able to run faster than a baboon, and he easily stayed out of her reach. He knew that she was a woman who was afraid of water, so he ran straight to the river. But when he came to the river bank he saw at once that he himself would never be able to cross it either, so he quickly changed himself into a wooden club.

Mother Baboon saw the club lying there. *Yo,* it was a beautiful club! She picked it up and talked to herself. She said to herself that it was the club with which she was going to kill Rabbit. But, while she held it, the club suddenly became such an ugly club that Mother Baboon threw it away. She threw it right across the river.

As soon as it landed on the opposite bank, it grew legs, and it became Rabbit again. He laughed, he laughed, he laughed, and the mountains laughed with him.

But Mother Baboon did not laugh. She wept. She wept over the five children that she and Rabbit had eaten every day.

Now Rabbit ran down the river bank. He jumped, he ran, he laughed. Then he came to Frog. Frog was playing on his flute. *Koo-rooo! koo-rooo!*

Mutla wanted the flute for himself. He said: "Well, fellow, you certainly have a flute there that cries very beautifully! Why don't you give it to me?" But Frog did not want to give his flute away.

But Rabbit really wanted that flute. He threw a handful of sand into Frog's eyes, and, when Frog dived into the water to wash his eyes, Rabbit picked up the flute that Frog had dropped beside the water. And he ran away, playing.

He ran until he came to Rock Hare. And Rock Hare was playing a flute that cried even more beautifully than the one that Rabbit had!

And now Mutla wanted that flute.

"Let us exchange, my brother," begged Rabbit. But Rock Hare did not want to. Then Rabbit invented a game to play with Rock Hare. They made a big fire, and then Rabbit told Rock Hare to throw him into the fire and take him out again at once. Then he would throw Rock Hare in and take him out at once.

It seemed a very nice game to Rock Hare, who was rather stupid. He threw Rabbit in and took him out so quickly that his fur was not even scorched, and then Rabbit threw Rock Hare into the fire. But before he did so, he said:

"Wait, my brother. Let me hold your flute for you." Hlolo gave him the flute, and as soon as Mutla held it in his hands he threw Hlolo into the fire and did not take him out again at all. He let him burn up altogether, and then he walked away, carrying Hlolo's flute with him. Then he blew on the flute and sang a song:

Piiiii, piiiii, Hlolo is a little boy,
He burns, but I come out,
I burn him and he dies!
Piiiii, piiiii, Hlolo is a little boy.
And this is the end of the story.

15. The Milk Tree

They tell of a brother and sister who lived long ago. The boy was called Hlabakuane and the girl was called Thakáne. They were the children of Rahlabakuane and Mahlabakuane. And at the hut of these people grew Kumonngu, the tree of the milk.

One day it happened that the parents went early to the fields. Hlabakuane had to take the cattle to the veld, and Thakáne had to take care of the hut and the milk tree, Kumonngu.

When she was alone in the shelter she heard the cows lowing. The sound did not come from the grazing ground: the lowing came from the corral. The cows lowed. They lowed. They lowed.

It was an ugly business. Where was the herder? She called him and said, "*Heela*, you, boy! *Ná*—where are you?"

He replied: "Here I am lying, in the shade of the trees."

"Do you not hear the lowing of the cows, *ná*? Do you not see them waiting for you so that you can take them to graze? See how high the sun has climbed already!"

"I have ears, child of my mother," he answered. "I hear them lowing, Thakáne. But I am not going to open the gate of that corral made of branches until I have drunk from Kumonngu, until I have his milk in my stomach."

"How can you talk like that, Hlabakuane?" asked the girl. "You know that Kumonngu is the food of our father, of our mother!"

"It does not matter," he replied. "I shall not take the cattle to the veld until I have drunk of the milk of that tree."

Thakáne heard the cattle lowing in the corral and she feared her father's displeasure. Then she cut a small slit in the bark of Kumonngu and tapped a small calabash of the sweet, thick milk for her brother.

She brought it to him and said: "Here is milk for you, milk from Kumonngu. Drink it quickly, so that you can take the cattle to graze."

But he was not satisfied. He did not want the milk. He turned his head away. "Such a little, little bit? If I do not get a big clay pot full of the milk of Kumonngu, the cattle will stay in the corral until the sun stands on those mountains in the west."

Yo na na wheh! Oh me, oh my! Here is great trouble! If Rahlabakuane should hear the lowing, he will come to see what is going on, and he will beat the herder with his stick! With the stick, the *molamu*!

She did not know what to do. She did not know, she did not know, and the cows kept lowing "*mooo-mooo! mooo-mooo!*"

Then she took a large clay pot and a sharp flint. With the flint she made a deep cut in the bark of Kumonngu. When the bark opened, the milk flowed out and she caught it in the large pot made of clay.

She filled the clay pot. Now, she thought, the milk would stop flowing. But it kept on, it kept on, it kept on.

It made a stream—a stream of milk! It grew wider! It grew

longer! It streamed over the veld! It streamed, and the fear of Thakáne was very great, because she could not stop the stream.

The man and the woman saw the broad stream of milk flowing toward them. They went to it. They dipped their hands in the milk of Kumonngu and drank of it. They drank and drank, and when their stomachs were full the stream turned round. It turned round and flowed back to the milk tree.

But now the man was very angry. The person who had opened Kumonngu must be punished, he said.

When he came to his home he asked his children: "*Ná*, who is he who broke the bark of Kumonngu?"

"It is she, Father, it is Thakáne," said the boy, because he was a bad person. His heart was not right.

"Is he speaking the truth, child of mine?" asked the mother, and the girl answered, "He speaks the truth, *Mè*."

Now her father's wrath was great over Thakáne. He decided to let her case be heard by the great council of the chief.

Her heart was black, because she knew that the chief was a *limo*. She knew that he ate people.

The heart of the mother was black also, because she knew she would never see her child again. Then she prepared Thakáne very nicely. After she had washed her body, she rubbed her face with fat, she rubbed fat on her arms, and she rubbed fat on her legs. She put her most beautiful clothes on Thakáne. She hung her most beautiful blanket round the shoulders of Thakáne. She gave her beautiful rings for her arms and legs, she gave her beautiful beads for her neck.

Aaaaa! Then she was beautiful! As bright as the sun, she, Thakáne!

Now she had to walk behind her father to the *khotla*, to the council of the chief. He walked in front. She walked behind. They walked in the footpath.

When they came by the fields where the wheat grew high enough to hide a clay pot, a steenbuck came running through the wheat. He saw the man and the girl, and he asked: "*Ná*, big man, where are you taking that child of yours who is so beautiful, so beautiful?"

He answered: "Ask her yourself. She has her years." The little buck did so. Then Thakáne answered him with a sad song:

> I give to my brother of Kumonngu,
> The herder of our cattle, Kumonngu,
> They stood in the corral till late, Kumonngu,
> Then I gave him my father's Kumonngu.

The steenbuck knew that the footpath along which the man and the girl were walking led to the maneaters. He felt very sorry for the girl and said to the man: "Rahlabakuane, it would be better if the *limo* ate you and let your child live."

Then they walked farther. The man walked in front, the girl walked behind him in the footpath. Just as they went through a muddy bog, they met an eland. He also asked: "*Ná*, big man, where are you taking that child of yours who is so beautiful, so beautiful?"

He replied: "She did a bad thing at my home. Ask her, she has her years."

Also for him Thakáne sang the song that was so sad.

"*Aaaaa!*" said the eland. "Rahlabakuane, it would be better if the *limo* ate you and allowed your child to live."

Then they walked farther. The man walked in front, the girl walked behind him in the footpath.

When it was night, they slept in the veld. Here they found a springbuck, and he also asked: "*Ná*, big man, where are you taking this child of yours who is so beautiful, so beautiful?"

Then Rahlabakuane replied with the same words that he had used to the steenbuck and the eland. Just so. *Yoalo*. And Thakáne answered him with the same sad song of the milk tree. *Yoalo*. *Yoalo*.

When the morning grew light, they walked farther. The man walked in front, the girl walked behind him in the footpath until they came to the place where the maneaters live.

Masilo was the son of the chief, but he did not eat people. When he saw the girl who waited so sadly at the *khotla* with her father, he spread an oxhide on the ground for her, but the father had to sit on the bare ground. Then he asked: "*Ná*, big man, why do you bring this girl who is so beautiful, so beautiful, here to my father? *Ná?*"

Then he answered the young man as he had answered the steenbuck, the eland, and the springbuck. "Ask her, she has her years."

And Thakáne answered him also with the sad song of Kumonngu, the sad song of the milk tree.

Masilo fell in love with her. And he said: "Rahlabakuane, it would be better if my father ate you and allowed the girl to live. She who is so beautiful, so beautiful."

Then he took the girl to the hut of his mother, but he sent his men to take the father to the mountain so that the maneaters could eat him there.

They killed him and cooked his body in a pot. They made meat out of him and ate it all up.

But the soul of that man did not die. It escaped from his body. It became a great rock, a *lefika*, that lay near the hut where the milk tree grew.

And then Masilo married Thakáne. They loved each other very much. Their joy was great. But when the first child was born, there was no joy, because the child was a girl. Because it was the custom of this tribe that no girl baby should live, when it is the firstborn of its parents.

The mother of Masilo told this to the mother of the child. She said: "The girl child is not allowed to live. The grave of the child will be the stomach of the *limo*."

Then Thakáne wept. She wept and refused to give up her child. She said: "It will be the mother herself who will seek a grave for her beloved. I would rather put her away in the water. This is my child, she is rejected by her father."

Then she tied the little one on her back in the *thari*, the carrying skin, and walked with her to the big river. And, where the deep pool of water shone in the sun between the reeds, there Thakáne sat down on the ground and she wept. She wept over her child, the girl baby who was rejected by her father and the people of his tribe.

As she sat weeping the water began to froth, the reeds began to shiver, and a woman appeared between the reeds. She asked, "Why do you weep, young woman?"

And Thakáne replied: "I weep for this little child! Among the people where I married, a girl child is not allowed to live when she is the firstborn. I brought her so that I could bury her in the water."

Then the old one comforted her. She said: "*Tula*, quiet, child of mine. It is I who will help you. Underneath this pool is my home. There I live in safety, and there I will keep and protect your child for you. And when your heart longs to see her, then you call to me from the edge of the pool, and I shall bring her to you."

Now the heart of Thakáne was glad. She gave the little one to the old woman and went back to Masilo. Then she told him that she had taken the child that he had rejected and buried her in the water. Just so. *Yoalo*.

Masilo and his tribesmen were satisfied, for so it had to happen in his tribe. So it had to be. It was right. And, every time that the heart of the mother longed for her child, she stood at the edge of the deep pool and sang the song of the little rejected one.

Bring here Lilahloane, that I might see her,
Little rejected one, rejected by Masilo . . .

Then the water would begin to froth. Then the reeds would begin to shiver, and then the old one would appear with the child on her back. Then the heart of Thakáne would be filled with joy, for she would have her child with her. And when it became time for her to go back to the house of Masilo, then the old woman would come back and fetch Lilahloane, to take her once again to the home deep under the pool that shone in the sunlight among the reeds.

Lilahloane grew well. She grew into a young girl, and the old one taught her to do all the work of a young girl. She also prepared her for marriage. With wisdom and good sense she instructed her, just as all the other girls of her years were instructed. And when she had finished the learning period of the young girls, the old one gave her the skin robe of the novice to put on, and one day, when Thakáne again came to visit her, the old one brought Lilahloane forth from beneath the water, clad in the skin robe.

Mè wheh, she looked just like the father who had rejected her! Just like Masilo! Just so!

While the mother and the child sat together by the pool, a man came to cut reeds to make a shelter in front of his hut. He saw the girl, he saw that she looked just like Masilo, and he knew that the child was the child of the *morena*, the master.

Then he ran to Masilo and told him what he had seen. He said: "*Morena*, it is she! The little rejected one!"

Then Masilo also went to the pool. He hid among the reeds and he saw them sitting and talking by the pool that shone in the sunlight among the reeds. He saw the water froth, he saw the reeds shiver, and then the old woman came out of the water to fetch the girl.

After Lilahloane had disappeared under the water with the old woman, Masilo went back to his home. He went to sit inside the shelter in front of his hut and he wept. He wept over his child.

When Thakáne came home she saw her husband's eyes were wet with tears, and she asked: "*Ná, Morena*, master, why are you crying, *ná*?"

But he answered with an untruth: "The dust blew in my eyes."

She believed him, but that night, when it was dark, she heard him crying as he lay on his sleeping mat. She asked, "Masilo, *ná*, what is wrong?"

And he answered: "My eyes have seen the little rejected one. My heart desires to have her back."

Then he slept. But when Thakáne heard him snoring *hò-na*,

hò-na, hò-na, she rose softly, and in the dark she ran to the river, because she was afraid for the safety of her child.

Mè wheh! Mè wheh! Now they will bury the child in the stomach of the *limo! Mè wheh! Mè wheh!*

She wept there by the side of the dark pool that lay sleeping among the reeds. She wept as she called the old woman with the song of the little rejected one. The old one heard her, and when she came out of the water Thakáne told her what had happened. But she said: "If the heart of the father is filled with longing for his child, he will not allow the maneaters to bury her!"

Thakáne said: "Grandmother, with you my child was safe!"

The old one answered with wisdom: "If there is love in the heart of the father, the child will be safe with him too. But I will not give this child to the father before he has taken out a hundred and again a hundred head of cattle from his herd for her."

Now Thakáne went back. Her heart was at ease. She went to lie down on the mat in the dark, and she slept as her husband did. But when it grew light Masilo awoke, and he began to weep again.

Then Thakáne spoke to him. She said: "The old woman sent a message to you. She said she will give your child back to you if you bring her a hundred head of cattle and again a hundred."

Chè, that was right. Masilo's heart was full of gratitude, and he sent his subjects to go and take a hundred head of cattle from his herd, and again a hundred.

He drove the cattle down to the river. The whole tribe wondered what was going on. And when the *morena* drove the herd of cattle, they all followed, so that their eyes could see what was to happen.

Such a thing they had never beheld before! *Yo!* See what Masilo is doing! He drove the cattle into the water! And when the hundred animals and again a hundred had disappeared into the depths, the old woman brought the beautiful young girl to her parents.

The sun grew dim and it grew dark around them, so beautiful

was she. And when her feet touched the bank of the river the sun shone again.

And before the eyes of the whole of his tribe Masilo took the little rejected one to his house again. Everybody's heart was full of joy, but one thing bothered Thakáne: she knew that Masilo had never given the cattle to her parents that he owed them for her, the mother of his child.

Chè, this was a matter that Masilo understood. By this neglect dishonor was brought to the woman of his house, the mother of his child. And he decided to take the cattle at once to the grandmother of his child. To her, to the woman who lived where the milk tree grew.

Now they gathered together a large company to undertake the journey. They took the cattle that was the bride price for Thakáne, they took pack oxen and pack horses. On the pack animals they put gifts of clay pots, skin blankets, mats, and iron utensils, and also food for the journey.

There were men who had to protect them from danger along the way. There were women who had to carry things on their heads.

And with them walked Mohlonkanyane, the little man who was smaller than the smallest child, who never grew any bigger, but who was cleverer than his own father, right from the day of his birth.

No, it was a big company. They walked, they walked, but right in front walked Thakáne, because of them all only she knew the way, the way back to the hut of Kumonngu.

But before they reached the hut of her mother, the woman saw a large boulder right in their way. A big *lefika*! This boulder was not always here!

It was quite incomprehensible!

Yo, then spoke the great *lefika*. He spoke with the voice of her father Rahlabakuane. He said:

"You walk in front, Thakáne, my child,
   I am going to eat you, and then the others."
Now Thakáne knew that her father had not yet forgiven her for breaking the bark of Kumonngu. And when that great *lefika* opened his mouth to swallow her, they quickly drove some of the cattle into it. But he was not yet satisfied.

"You walk in front, Thakáne, my child,
   I am going to eat you, and then the others."
Then he opened his mouth again for his child, but then they drove the pack oxen into it. After all the cattle had been devoured, they would have to give the people to the *lefika*.

He swallowed all the people.

Yo na na wheh! Inside the stomach of the *lefika* it was dark! Dark as a cave deep in a canyon! It was dark. It was very dark, and there they sat with the pack oxen and the cattle that the boulder had swallowed before.

Now Mohlonkanyane, that little man who was smaller than an infant, made a plan, because he was wiser and cleverer than the oldest men.

He hacked a door in the wall of the stomach of the *lefika*, and it was rock that splintered as he hacked.

He hacked, he hacked, he hacked, until there was an opening, a door big enough for him, the little man, and the animals and the people to walk through and escape.

They did so. Only the animals that the rock had swallowed long before Thakáne and her company came there stayed inside the *lefika*. And, when everybody was outside again, they went to greet the mother of Thakáne. They greeted her with the gifts they had brought for her. They gave her the cattle for her daughter Thakáne, and they showed her the child of her child, Lilahloane.

Now the joy was great in that village by the milk tree. They had a feast. So big a feast no one of the guests had ever seen, and so we come to the end of the story.

16. Jackal and Hen

This is a story that the old people tell.

They say that Hen flew to the top of a stack of wheat one day to find food. From where she stood on the stack she could see far out over the fields. She could see far, and she saw Jackal coming from afar. She saw him coming toward her, she saw him out of the corner of her eye, but when he came closer she did not look up at all. She went on hunting for food.

"Good morning, mother of mine," Jackal greeted her.

"Yes, I greet you," she replied.

"Are you still living?" he asked, according to the correct way in which one person greets another.

"Yes, I am still living. And you? Are you still living also?"

"Yes, I too am still living, Mother," he replied. And then he asked, as the custom was, "Did you wake well this morning?"

And she answered, as it is proper, "Yes, I woke well."

And all the while he was talking, talking, talking, Jackal was looking closely at Hen, and he saw that she was young and that her flesh would be tender and that she would taste sweet if only he could get at her. But now she was standing on top of that stack of wheat, where he could not reach her. He could not get hold of her at all, not while she was on top of the stack of wheat, and he would have to think of a way to get her down.

Jackal had many plans. He was a man who was not just a little bit clever. No, he was very clever. Very clever. He asked her: "Mother, have you heard that there is peace among everybody on earth? One animal may not catch another animal any more, because of that peace."

"Peace?" she asked.

"Yes, Mother, peace. The chiefs called together a big meeting, and at that *pitso* they decided this business of peace on all the earth."

"Oh yes," said Hen. But she wondered about it. She wondered whether this Jackal could be telling the truth. He was a man with many clever stories, and many times those clever stories were nothing but lies.

"You say there is peace now?"

"Yes, Mother. The big peace. There has never been such a big peace. You can safely come down from that stack of wheat. Then we can talk about the matter nicely. We shall take snuff together. Come down, Mother! Remember the peace!"

But Hen was not quite as stupid as Jackal thought she was. She wanted to make quite sure first that Jackal was telling the truth and that he was not telling her lies again. She turned around and looked far out over the fields behind her. Then she went to stand on the highest point of the stack and kept staring out over the fields until Jackal asked: "What is it that you see from up there that you stare so, *Mè*?"

"What do I see? Why do you want to know what I see? It does not matter what I see, for there is no danger any more for any animal on earth. Is it not peace among the animals? It is only a pack of dogs that are running toward us."

"Dogs! A pack of dogs!" he cried. And his fear was very great. "Then I shall have to greet you, Mother. I am a man who has a lot of work waiting."

"*Kêkêkêkê!*" Hen laughed. "I thought it was peace among all animals on earth? Have you forgotten it? The dogs will do nothing to harm you! Why do you want to run away, Grandfather?"

"I don't think that this pack of dogs came to the meeting of the peace!" And Jackal ran so fast that the dust rose in great clouds from the road behind him.

"*Kêkêkêkê!*" laughed Hen, for then she knew that the story of the peace was just a big lie. And she knew that if she had taken snuff with that fellow he would have caught her, so she made up a story herself and with it she had caught him beautifully.

"*Kêkêkêkê!*" she laughed. "I caught the storyteller with another story!"

And this is the end of this story.

17. The Whirlwind and the Land
   of the Half-men

They tell of Ntotoatsana, who was the daughter of a chief. She and her brother were the only children of that big man. It was just the two of them: the boy child and the girl child.

But he had much cattle, did that chief, and when it was summer he told Ntotoatsana that she must help her brother herd the cattle, for he could not tend them alone as they were too many. Altogether too many.

She obeyed her father, and she walked with her brother behind the cattle as they went to graze. But her heart was black, for it is not woman's work to tend cattle. It is man's work. But she said nothing. She kept quiet. *Tu-u-u-u* . . .

Her brother walked on one side of the herd, she walked on the other side, and he did not know at all that her heart did not want to lie down. He did not know it at all.

They walked, they walked, they walked. When the herd was grazing peacefully, he walked to some other herders and talked with them. But she was too ashamed that they should see her, so she sat down behind a clump of broomgrass.

No one saw her sitting there. Not even her brother. But Setsokot-sane, the whirlwind, who whirls *tsoko, tsoko, tsoko* over the veld, saw her sitting there, crouched like a little partridge hiding from a hawk.

Tsoko, tsoko, tsoko he whirled closer to her. He sang to her, she listened to him. He danced for her and she watched.

He came up to her. He lifted her from the ground and carried her away. Very far away, to the land of his master.

His master was a man of the Matabele tribe, but he was not a whole man. He was only half a man. He had only one ear and one eye. He had only one arm and one leg. He did not walk like other people, he hopped on that one leg. That is how he walked.

And in front of the hut of this man Setsokotsane, the whirlwind, put down this beautiful daughter of a chief, for this man had no wife.

Yo whch, now the heart of Ntotoatsana was blacker than ever, for she did not want to be the wife of the half-man. But she could do nothing about it, she could only weep. She wept the whole day. And the night also. She could not stop weeping.

Half-man gave her many clothes, he had a beautiful home built for her, and he put many jackal skins on its floor. But her heart remained black, it did not want to lie down. When Half-man asked her with his half-mouth why her eyes were so red, she replied that it was the smoke from the fire that hurt them. *Yoalo.* Just so.

One night, when it was dark and her husband was asleep, and Whirlwind was not walking around any more, she hung her blanket over her shoulders and crept cautiously out through the door of the hut. She crept along the reed screen in front of the hut until she came to its opening. She crept so quietly that the dog did not even stir in its sleep.

She wanted to flee from that half-man. She wanted to go back to the home of her parents. But, just as she was going out through the opening in the screen, she heard the sound of a horn coming from in-

side the hut. It called the man who was sleeping so peacefully, and
it said:

U-u-u-u! Setsokotsane, the whirlwind, brings the woman,

She runs away, the one who herded cattle, *U-u-u-u!*

The man awoke, he put his hand out to the sleeping mat beside
his. *Chè*, the horn of a ram that he had buried beneath the floor of
the hut did not wake him up in vain.

Ntotoatsana had fled.

He hopped, hopped, hopped after her in the dark, he grabbed her
and brought her back to the sleeping mat. Hop, hop, hop.

"You will never be able to run away from me," he said to her.
"Whirlwind has brought you, and Horn is guarding you. He will
call me every time that you run away. As he did tonight. *Yoalo,
yoalo, yoalo.*"

And so it was. Ntotoatsana could not flee. She could not. She
could not. She must stay in that land where all the men looked like
her husband. As though they had been cut in half from their heads
down.

After a while she had children: twins. They were girls. *Yo!* they
were beautiful! They looked just like their mother, Ntotoatsana.
They had two little eyes and two little ears. They had two little
arms and two little legs. They did not hop, they walked.

When Ntotoatsana saw that her children were born right, her
heart went to lie down. She did not try to flee any more, for the
horn-that-called was still buried in the floor of her house.

One day the two children walked down to the spring to fetch
water. And when they came there, they saw a strange man standing there. Two eyes, two ears, two arms, two legs! *Yo!*

"We greet you, Father," they said, politely.

He greeted them also. "Whose children are you?" he said, "that
you are completely whole in this land of half-people? Whole, with
all your eyes and your ears and your arms and your legs? *Ná?* Why
do you look different?"

"We look like our mother," they said.

"Who is your mother?"

"A woman that Setsokotsane, the whirlwind, brought here. Her name is Ntotoatsana."

Then the man was glad. Very glad, for she was his sister for whom he had been searching for many years. He was glad, but he said nothing to the girls. He kept quiet. *Tu-u-u* . . .

The head of this brother of Ntotoatsana was soft, so he thought up a good way to talk with his sister: he pulled a good, strong reed from the ground and cut a flute for each child. When he gave them the flutes, he said: "When you get home, go to your mother and ask her for buttermilk. When she gets up from the skin on which she is sitting to go and get the milk for you inside the house, then you must hide the flutes under the skin."

He told them, they listened.

He told them, they listened well. And when they got to their house, they did as he had told them to do. Just so. *Yoalo.*

After their mother had given them the buttermilk she went back to that skin. But as she sat down, the reed flutes broke under her: *twaa, twaa!*

Then those two little girls cried! They cried so hard that it sounded like dogs howling when the light of the moon falls on the earth. They cried over their reed flutes, for that was what the stranger at the spring had told them to do.

"Quiet, quiet, my children!" comforted Ntotoatsana. "I will send a young man to fetch another reed. Then we shall make new flutes for you."

"No," they said, "no, you must go and fetch the reed yourself. You broke the flutes, you must fetch the reed."

They were doing as the man by the spring had told them to do.

The mother did not want her children to be so sad, so she went down to the spring to fetch a reed. She walked, she got there. And when she looked up, she saw her brother standing among the reeds.

Yo, she was glad!

"Where do you come from, child of our house?" she asked. "Are you still alive?"

"Yes, I am still alive," he replied, "but it is many long years that we search for you. Our mother has never again cut her hair, for she mourns for you, she thinks you are dead. But now I have finished searching. Bring your possessions and your children, so that we can go home."

"*Chè*," she said. "That cannot happen. Just as I want to flee, the horn tells it to my husband."

"This horn, which one is it?"

"The horn of a ram, that sleeps in the floor of my hut. It can talk, even though no one is blowing at its end. It says:

U-u-u-u! Setsokotsane, the whirlwind, brought the woman,
She runs away, the one who herded cattle, *U-u-u!*"

But that brother of Ntotoatsana was clever. He said: "When horn-that-calls sleeps, it cannot call its master. Then it cannot call its master when you flee, *ná*? Can it?"

"It never sleeps. It is a horn that is always awake. In the night. In the day. Always."

"If it is drunk, it will sleep," said the brother. "You must make it drunk, that horn who is such a tell-tale."

"How can I make it drunk, *ná!*" said she. "You don't know that horn, you don't know its master."

"My sister, listen. You must pour the dregs of very strong beer into that horn until its stomach is full. Then you must stop its mouth up with clay. You must push the clay in tightly and deeply, so that the beer cannot run out. Then you must put the horn back in its old place, so that it can sleep. That is what you must do."

When the sun went down Ntotoatsana buried the horn with its stomach full of beer in the floor. *Yoalo, yoalo*. And after he had finished eating, that husband of hers slept. But she lay awake until that heart of hers told her that the horn was sleeping very deeply.

Then she took her children and fled to the spring where her brother waited for her among the reeds.

When the dark of that night became light, they were already far away from the land of the half-people. Now they did not go any farther, for they were afraid that Setsokotsane might see them and take them back to his master. They crept into the bushes and waited for the dark of the following night. So they went. Only in the dark.

They walked for ten nights and another two nights before they came to the village of their father. There was great rejoicing when the parents saw their children and their grandchildren. They made a great feast with the flesh of many oxen and many sheep and much beer. The mother shaved off her hair that had grown as long as the tail of a bird. And this is the end of the story.

Ke tsomo ka mathetho, which means: this is a true tale of the Basotho people.

18. Nanabolele, Who Shines in the Night

Long long ago, when the parents of our grandparents were still children, there were three orphans: two boy children and their sister, Thakáne. Their father had been a great chief when he was alive. But now he was dead, and it was Thakáne who had to take care of her two brothers.

She had to grind corn for them and make the porridge. She had to cook the meat that they brought back from the hunt. She had to fill the clay pots with water so that they did not have to drink from the spring like dogs.

She took care of them like a mother.

But when the time came that the two boys had to go to the tribal school, the school to which fathers take their sons so that they may become men, it was Thakáne who took them to the school. It was Thakáne who took them to the school, for they no longer had a father who could take them. According to the traditions of the tribe they stayed in the grass huts of the school for the required five months, and, when the time was spent, it was Thakáne who prepared their clothes and their skin shields and their weapons.

It was she who took the clothes to them to the huts in the mountains when all the fathers took clothes to their sons. It was she who took the clothes so that they could be loosened from those grass huts, the *mophato*. It was she.

But when her brothers saw the clothes they refused to accept them. They said that they would stay inside those grass huts until the day came that they each received a *karos*—a skin blanket—a cap, a skin to hang around the hips, and a skin shield made of the skin of the nanabolele, those horrible creatures who give off light in the dark, as the moon and the stars give off light in the dark. The nanabolele who lived beneath the waters.

"Why do you ask for the impossible?" asked the young woman. "Where shall I find the skin of the nanabolele? Where? *Ná?*"

But the two young men would not listen to her. They said if their father had still been alive it would have been the skins of those big monsters that would have loosened them from the huts of the school. It did not become them, the sons of a chief, to be loosened from the huts in the same way as all the others, with the same clothes. They, who were the boy children of a great chief who was dead, ought to have much finer loosening clothes.

Then word went out from Thakáne, and it was spread, spread, spread around until all the subjects of the chief had heard it. She called her people together.

When they who had been summoned sat together in the big gathering, the *pitso*, Thakáne opened her heart to them. She said: "You must choose among yourselves the bravest of all, so that they can walk with me when I go to find the nanabolele."

"*Yo wheh!*" they said. "How can you, who are only a woman, undertake such a dangerous task?"

But she answered, "If the father of my brothers had lived, his sons would have had clothes made from the skins of the nanabolele."

Chè, now they understood.

They gathered together a band of the bravest of them all. The women prepared food to take along, food for a very long journey. They took flesh of oxen, flesh of sheep, ground wheat, calabashes full of beer, and cooked corn balls that were made of ground sweet corn. Everything was loaded on the backs of pack oxen.

It was a very large company, with many pack oxen, that set off that day with Thakáne when she left her home to seek the dragons with the shiny skins, the dragons that lived beneath the waters.

When they came to the first stream, they saw that it was broad. Perhaps the nanabolele were beneath the waters of this stream . . . they did not know. They took the hindquarters of an ox and threw it in the water. Then Thakáne sang. She called with this song:

Nanabolele, nanabolele!
The sons of the chief, nanabolele!
They want shields, nanabolele!
Shoes from the skin of nanabolele!
Blankets from the skin of nanabolele!
And hats from the skin of nanabolele!

When she had finished singing, the waters began to move. They trembled. They churned. *Kattay, kattay, kattay!*

They were afraid, for they thought it was one of the monsters. But only a frog jumped out. He cried: "*Koo-rooo, koo-rooo, koo-rooo,* go farther. There where you can dip water with the husk of the poison plant, there you must cross."

They obeyed the frog, and, when they had crossed the stream, they walked farther until they reached the next stream. Here the water flowed broad and calm. Maybe it was deep also, they did not know. Maybe it was under those waters that the nanabolele lived. And again Thakáne sang and told of her search and what her mission was, as she had done by the first stream. Just so. *Yoalo.*

When she had finished singing, the waters began to tremble. They churned. *Kattay, kattay!* Again they thought it was the nanabolele, but as at the first stream only a frog leaped out, and he also cried: "*Koo-rooo, koo-rooo,* go farther. There where you can dip water with the husk of the poison plant, there you must cross." Just so. *Yoalo.*

At every stream the same thing happened, and they did not find the monsters with the shining skins. Then they came to the last river. The reeds grew high and thick on its banks, and the river was wider than all the others. Perhaps it was deeper also. They did not know, and maybe it would be beneath these waters that they would find the nanabolele.

They threw meat into the waters, but the river lay still. The waters did not tremble, they did not churn, they lay still.

Thakáne sang the song of the sons of the chief who had to have clothes made of the shining skins of the nanabolele, but the waters did not move. They threw meat into the water, but the waters lay still. They threw meat in again, but the waters lay still. Then they killed a pack ox and threw it in whole. Again Thakáne sang the song to the nanabolele, and as she sang the waters began to move. They trembled, they churned, they welled up over the banks, they boiled like water over a very big fire. It was surely the monsters with their shining skins, they thought, and the men stood ready with their spears. But still it was not a monster, it was a very old woman who appeared. She leaned on a stick and invited them to follow her.

Then she went back into the waters, and the whole company dived in after her. Under the dark waters, under the thick reeds, they came to a big village. They were amazed, for it looked like the village of a mighty chief. Here were also huts with reed screens in front of them, and it was dry as it was dry above the ground. But still it was different, for the village was quite deserted. It was quiet. No people lived there. No children were playing there. The huts stood empty. There were no fires behind the screens. The clay pots were without water. The grinding stones lay idle.

"*Mè wheh!*" said Thakáne and her people. "Such a strange place we have never seen! Where then are the people, Grandmother?"

She replied: "They are all dead, the nanabolele ate them all, the adults and the children, the cattle and the sheep, the dogs and the chickens. Everything!"

"And you, Grandmother?" they asked.

"No, my children, I am too old. My flesh is too tough from much work through the years, and I am too thin. That is why these awful monsters have saved my life, so that I can work for them. I heard your song, young woman," said she. "You dare much!"

"*Yo wheh!* Now I see the danger is great," said Thakáne, because she suspected that the old one had lured them into a trap to supply food for her monsters, but the old woman reassured them and hid them in a deep, dark hole that she covered over with reeds and soil so that the nanabolele should not see them.

And just as they were well hidden they heard a roaring above their heads, a roaring like a huge herd of oxen passing over the ground. . . . It was the nanabolele.

Dooma, dooma, dooma, they dived into the water and came to the deserted village beneath the dark waters that flowed among the reeds. They came to sleep, for they were weary from hunting.

Thakáne and her people peeped through the reeds. *Yo-yo-yo!* It was frightening! They saw a whole herd of dragons coming closer in the dark . . . *foo-foo-foo!* They shone! The skins gave off light as the moon and stars give off light at night. But they did not go to sleep, they walked around. They were looking for something. They put their noses to the ground and smelled. They sniffed: *foo-foo!*

Then they spoke. They said, "We smell the stink of people!" Then they searched through the empty huts, but they found nothing. And the old woman remained silent. *Tu-u-u . . .*

"*Sentho se nkha kae?*" they asked. "Where does that stink of human flesh come from?"

Then they searched, searched, searched, but they were so weary from hunting that they could stay awake no longer. They would sleep first, and the next day they would search again and find out where the stink came from.

As soon as they were asleep and snoring fearfully loudly, the old one came to fetch Thakáne and her people from their hiding place and told them that they must quickly choose one of the nanabolele and slaughter and skin it before the others woke up.

They did so. They chose the largest one, and when they had skinned it they rewarded the grandmother with pack oxen laden with food. Then they had to leave.

But first the old one gave Thakáne a little ironstone pebble and said: "Tomorrow, when the nanabolele wake up and see that you have killed one of them, they will follow your spoor."

"*Yo wheh!*" groaned the people.

But she continued: "As soon as you see red dust clouds against the sky you will know that the nanabolele are following you. Then you must put that pebble down in the road. It will grow, it will grow until it is a high mountain. Then you must climb up on that mountain before it is too high. On top of that mountain there will be asylum for you."

So they took the skin of the nanabolele and left that village under the dark waters, the village asleep with all the monsters, the village where only one old woman lives, she who takes care of the nanabolele.

It was still dark when Thakáne and her company arrived above the ground again. They did not wait for the light, for they were in a great hurry to leave. Only when they had gone a long way toward their homes did the dark grow light. And it was still early in the day when they saw the red clouds rising against the sky behind them. And they knew it was the dust that the dragons were raising as they pursued Thakáne and her people.

They who were fleeing were afraid!

But when the dust clouds appeared around the last mountain

peak, Thakáne quickly put the pebble down on the ground. And then it grew. They climbed up on it, and it grew, grew, grew. It became a mountain that touched the clouds. And on top of that mountain Thakáne and her company sat in safety. When the herd of nanabolele arrived at the mountain they tried to clamber up, but they could not climb up, for those mountainsides were of ironstone, and they were steep and they were slippery.

When the monsters were so tired from struggling that they could struggle no longer, they lay down on the ground at the foot of the mountain to rest. But they were so exhausted that they fell asleep immediately—and then that mountain of ironstone began to shrink. It grew smaller, smaller, smaller, until again it was only a pebble that could be carried in the hand of a human.

Thakáne took that pebble and she and her company fled, carrying the skin of the nanabolele with them.

The same thing happened the next day. *Yoalo. Yoalo.* Every day. And every day Thakáne came closer to home with that shining skin, every day. Behind them, following their footprints in the road, came the herd of nanabolele, and above them the red dust clouds also came nearer.

But the people stayed in the lead, and when they reached their own village Thakáne quickly called all the dogs so that they should come and wait with her. And when the monsters came to the ash heaps of the village, Thakáne set the dogs on them.

This they did not expect. The dogs rushed to the attack, and the nanabolele came no closer. They came no closer, but turned round and went back to their deserted village, taking their red dust clouds with them. Back to the old woman who cared for them under the dark waters of the deep river that flows among the reeds.

Thakáne was satisfied. She had done her duty toward the children of that father of hers who was no longer alive, she had found the skin that gave off light like the moon and the stars when the sun does not shine any more.

Now she summoned a man who was skilled in the making of skin clothes. And from the skin of the nanabolele he cut two shields, two blankets, two hats, two hip cloths, and two pairs of shoes. And when the clothes were ready, Thakáne herself took them to her brothers, there where they waited in the *mophato* for their initiation into manhood, waited to be loosened from those huts.

The two young men were glad when they saw the shining clothes that their sister had brought them. Not one of the other young men who had attended the school with them had such clothes. Nobody had ever had such clothes. Not only the people of their own region, but also the people of the whole country, told each other of the shining shields, the shining blankets, the shining hats, the shining hip cloths, and the shining shoes that the brothers wore.

And above all the honor that they received for their clothes, above the honor was a great gratitude for their sister. That was why they rewarded her out of their herds. They gave her a hundred head of cattle, and here the story finds its end.

Ke tsomo ka mathetho, which means: this is a true tale of the Basotho people.

19. Sheep and Baboon

The old people know all about the hostility that still exists today between Sheep and Baboon, between Nkoe and Tsoene. When Sheep catches a glimpse of Baboon he runs away as fast as he can, for he knows, he knows that Baboon will catch him, will catch him and tear him apart.

The old people know how this business started. It was very long ago.

Nkoe, the sheep, was the young man, and he was very beautiful. His horns were long, they were sharp, and everybody was afraid of those horns. The fathers of his kind were all hoping that he would take cattle out of his herds for one of their daughters, but he said no, they were all too stupid. He wanted a clever girl for a bride. Clever, as the people who live in the mountains are clever.

He took a fancy to the daughter of Baboon. *Au*, she was very clever! She could do many things that a sheep could not do. She was just like a human being. She could climb trees and fetch food out of the branches of the trees. No, it was the daughter of Tsoene who should become his wife. It was she, the daughter of Baboon.

And so he went into the mountain country to Tsoene. He walked, he walked, he walked. Then he came to the cliff where Baboon lived. He came to that cliff. He greeted Tsoene as it becomes a young man to greet a big man, when he came to speak to him. At first he addressed the wealth of Baboon.

"Those cattle!" said Nkoe.

"Yes," said Tsoene and blinked his bright little eyes. "Yes!"

"Good day, Grandfather," said Sheep respectfully.

"Yes," said Tsoene. "Good day, Nkoe. What is the reason why you left your plains today to come and see me here in my mountains?"

Sheep opened his heart to Tsoene.

"I have many cattle, and I shall give you as many as you desire for that girl of yours," said Sheep, and he tossed his head as he spoke. Tsoene looked at his horns. Those long horns that lay curled against his head, with those sharp points.

It made Tsoene think very hard. He thought, he thought, he thought, and when he had finished thinking he spoke. He spoke and said: "*Chè*, Nkoe, I heard you. It is right so. If you would take fifty cattle from your herds and give me a horse so that I might ride when I take care of them, you may have this girl of mine."

"I hear you, great Chief, and I thank you." He tossed his head again and Tsoene again looked at those sharp horns. Then he said: "I have not finished speaking, Nkoe! I have a condition, and only on this condition can you have my daughter."

"What is your condition, Father of mine?" asked Sheep.

"You can take your wife. But you must move down to the plains, and you must never come back to my mountains. Never again. Never again."

"What is the reason for this, great Chief?" asked Sheep.

"It is those horns of yours. Such sharp horns are an ugly business. They can stick in my eyes and then I shall be blind."

"That is true," Sheep admitted. "That could happen."

"Yes, it could happen," said Baboon. "And that is why I never again want to see you here at my *kraal*, at my village."

"I understand this business, Grandfather Tsoene," said Sheep, and he took his bride. That clever daughter of Baboon. The clever woman who was cleverer than all the clever women in the *kraal* of Sheep.

But then trouble came. The wife of Sheep had a boy child. And then she wanted to go and show the little man to his grandfather in the mountains.

"Wife of mine," said Nkoe, "it cannot happen. There are many dangers hiding along the road. It is not safe for you and the child to walk so far alone."

"You must walk with me, Nkoe. You and your men must go with us. It is your horns that will protect me and the child on my back."

"Your father has said that I must not come near his *kraal*, and I gave him my word."

"That fire has burned itself out, father of my boy child."

"What do you mean when you speak so?"

"I want to tell you that those words have no strength any more. It is the ashes that remain after the fire has burned itself out."

Then Sheep understood and he called his men together so that they should go to the mountain country with his wife and their child. And when the company came to Tsoene, there was great trouble.

"What are you doing here with those sharp horns?" shouted Tsoene. "You want to come and stick them in my eyes so that I cannot see any more. That is what you have come to do! An agreement is an agreement. Words are not wood that burn out until they are destroyed!"

Tsoene called his other children to come and help him, and they attacked Nkoe and his men. Tsoene and his men won, because the sheep did not know the mountain country at all. Sheep took his wife and the little man, and together with his men he fled back to the plains.

And that was how the trouble began between Tsoene, the man who needed his eyes to see far out over the countryside, and Nkoe, the chief of the sheep of the plains below.

And that trouble exists to this very day. Sheep will never dare to go near Baboon. And Tsoene is still just as scared as ever that Sheep will stick his horns in his eyes and blind him. And if he gets hold of Sheep he will tear him apart.

And that is the end of the story.

20. The Woman with the Big Thumbnail

They tell of Machakatane. Her name tells you that she is a woman who does not stay at home. No, she wanders around. She is very rich, this woman. She has cattle. She has sheep. She has goats. But she does not slaughter any of her animals. The only flesh that she eats is flesh that is tender—the flesh of humans.

Everybody knew Machakatane. They feared her and hid when they heard that she was out hunting near them.

When you looked at her she was not ugly. No, she looked just like other women. There was only one thing that distinguished this maneater-woman from other women: it was a dreadful thing! It was the nail on the thumb of her right hand. It was very large. *Yo,* it was so big she could cover a human being with it, she could squeeze a person to the ground when she wanted to catch one.

Such a nail had never before been seen on the finger of any other person. And it was hard, that nail, so hard that it could protect its owner when a spear was thrown at her. *Chè,* when danger came close to Machakatane it was that nail that she used as a shield.

She went hunting often, this woman. She went far into the mountains and the regions beyond to hunt. And she killed so many people that she could not eat them all. She carried the corpses to her home and put them away in a hut that stood apart from the one in which she lived. It was the hut of her daughter, Sechakatane. She was a girl who was not yet married.

She had to sleep among those corpses. Every night. Every night. She shook with fear as she unrolled her sleeping mat among the dead ones, and with a heart full of terror she lay down and pulled her *karos*, her skin blanket, over her head. When she thought of the corpses she could not sleep.

And it was with that same frightened heart of the night before that she rose every morning. No, she had a hard life. She, Sechaka-tane. There were also no other people with whom she could talk. When Machakatane was out hunting she was alone in that big vil-lage, with all the empty houses, empty because her mother had eaten everybody who had lived there; the adults and the children and the babies. Everybody.

When the chief of that region heard of the murders that this woman had committed his anger was great. But he was a brave chief and decided to attack the maneater. *Yoalo*. Just so.

He called his warriors together. He called them together, and then he chose the bravest among them. They took their weapons and their dogs, and with their chief they drew up toward Machakatane.

They stalked her village. But they went no nearer than the deep canyon that cut through the mountains near her village. There the big man let his men hide among the bushes. They and their dogs. It was only he who walked alone to the village of the maneater. He walked very cautiously. He stayed above the wind, so say the old people, because you have to be very careful of anyone with such a big nail on the thumb.

When the chief approached the village, he listened. He listened, but he heard no sounds of people. A great silence lay among the huts. He peeped through the chinks in the reed screens in front of the huts to see what the people were doing, but he saw no one. It was empty behind the screens. And there were no fires burning. Everything was quiet. *Tu-u-u-u.*

Chief Bulane now knew that it had been the truth that he had heard about Machakatane: she had eaten all her own people, and that was why the village was empty, and silence reigned even inside the screens.

Hm! He did not know what to do. Where would he find that woman? He walked among the huts, and then he heard a woman's voice singing:

>   *Hiii-hiii-hiii-ai!*
>   *Hiii-hiii-hiii-ai!*

He went closer to the voice. It came from behind the screen in front of the biggest hut in the village. He went nearer. He went nearer. He went nearer.

He peeped through the reeds of the shelter. There he saw a girl sitting. She was beautiful, but she was very thin. She was black from thinness. It was she who sang so sadly:

>   *Hiii-hiii-hiii-ai!*
>   *Hiii-hiii-hiii-ai!*

He went in by the opening in the screen, and when she saw him she was frightened and wanted to flee like an animal that is startled from its sleep, but he talked nicely to her. He put her at ease, and when her heart had lain down Bulane again spoke to her. He asked politely:

"Who are you, Mother?"

And she replied: "I am the daughter of Machakatane, *Morena*, my master. But you must flee, Father. That woman will kill you for your flesh if she finds you here. It is nearly time for her to return."

But he said he would hide. He would wait for her. *Yoalo. Yoalo.*

"Where will you hide, *Morena*? Her nose will tell her that a human is here."

"I will sit in your sleeping hut, and then she will think it is you that she smells."

"*Au, Morena*, you cannot go in there. My hut is the place where the dead are kept, the meat for Machakatane!"

"*Chè*," said he, "then we must not look for another place for me to hide. The smell of my body will make friends with the smell of the dead ones. She will never know that a live person is sitting with her meat."

So say the old people. And, when the girl saw how brave he was and how wisely he spoke, her respect for him grew. When she heard the footfalls of Machakatane, she hid Bulane in the darkness of her hut, behind all the dead ones who were there.

Machakatane came there. She did not know of Bulane who sat so still with all the dead ones. She ate quickly and went out to hunt again.

When she had gone, the girl Sechakatane called to Bulane so that he could come out.

He did so, and then he went to the corrals where the cattle were, there where Machakatane's great herds were. He let them come out. All of them. And they were many, so say the old people. Bulane put Sechakatane on the back of an ox, and they drove the cattle to the canyon where his men were waiting for him.

But the way was long. And it was dry. The hoofs of the great herd of cattle loosened the hard-packed earth and sent great clouds of dust into the air. The maneater saw the red clouds against the sky. And she knew it was her cattle being driven away.

She did not wait. She followed them. So say the old people. She ran after them, and, when Sechakatane saw how the huge nail on her thumb reflected the rays of the sun like a pool of water, she became afraid, but Bulane calmed her.

"You must let your heart lie down, *Mè*," said he. I shall see that no harm comes to you."

When Machakatane came close to them, he caused a great row

of trees to appear between them, a row of trees that stretched all the way up the canyon. So say the old people.

Bulane and Sechakatane climbed into the tree nearest to them. When the old woman came to the tree she saw them sitting in the branches. She laughed, because she thought she had them in her power. She laughed, she laughed, and then she started to cut down the tree with that hard nail on her thumb. But just as the tree was about to fall, the two fugitives jumped into the tree that was the second tree in the row.

Machakatane saw them. She saw them and she began to cut down the trunk of that second tree also with her nail, just like the first one. *Yoalo.* Just so. But before she could catch Bulane and her daughter, they jumped into the branches of the next tree.

And so it kept on. So it kept on. Until the two fugitives sat in the last tree in the canyon. The maneater cut that trunk also with her nail. She did not know of the danger that waited for her. *Twah!* she cut. *Twah, twah!*

Then Bulane called to his men, who had been sitting as quietly as partridges between the bushes.

"Bring your dogs," he commanded. "Set them on that woman!"
They did so. *Yoalo. Yoalo.*

When the dogs attacked her she used that thumbnail of hers as a shield. She hid behind it, so say the old people. But it could not protect her. When the dogs were in front, the warriors would attack from behind. And, when she held the shield between herself and the warriors, the dogs would attack from behind. Just so. *Yoalo. Yoalo.*

They killed Machakatane. They killed her well, so that she could not come alive again. The dogs tore her apart and ate her flesh as she had eaten the flesh of so many people.

When the danger was over, Bulane took the young girl to his village. His wives fed her with much food and she grew fat. She was so fat she was yellow in the face. She shone, so beautiful was she. And Bulane divided the cattle of the maneater between her and himself. She was now not only a beautiful girl, but she also had much cattle.

Bulane's big *induna*, Bulane's big warrior chief, saw Sechakatane and loved her. He drove much cattle from his own herd to that of Bulane, to pay for Sechakatane. And the chief gave her to the *induna* as wife, so they say, because she did not have a father or a big brother who could give her away.

They held a great feast to celebrate the marriage of Sechakatane and the *induna*: many oxen and sheep were slaughtered, many clay pots of beer were brewed. And the young people danced and sang for many days and nights on end. Such a big feast had never been held in that land.

After the feast was over, the *induna* and his bride and many other people went back to the village of Machakatane, enough people to fill all the empty huts again. And they took their cattle with them, so say the old people. Enough cattle to fill all the empty corrals again.

The *induna* then became chief over all the people and of the whole territory that had belonged to the maneater-woman. And Sechakatane was his first and most important wife.

And here the story finds an end.

Ke tsomo ka mathetho, which means: this is a true tale of the Basotho people.

21. Tsananapa

The old people tell of a chief who had no boy children. He had only one daughter. They called her by the name of Tsananapa.

Her parents loved her very much. They took very good care of her, and the people of their village also all loved her very much. The old people loved her very much and the young people loved her very much.

Every day when the young girls went to the mountain to gather wood they came to fetch her so that she could go with them.

When they invited her, she would reply, "First you have to beg my mother to allow me to go." Then they would do so. They begged the mother to let Tsananapa go, and then the heart of the mother was at ease, for she knew that the girl children of that village would take good care of Tsananapa.

When they came to the place where they gathered wood, they would spread open their blankets in the shade so that she could sit on them. And, when she sat on the blankets, her little dog would lie down beside her.

Then the girls would bring Tsananapa all the food that they had brought with them. They would put it all in front of her, and she could choose, choose the food that she wanted to eat. She could eat just as much as she liked, she and her dog. Then the girls would eat the food that remained when Tsananapa and her dog had eaten their fill.

Then they would go and pick up kindling. But the darling of the house of the chief would remain sitting on the blankets. She and her little dog.

When the other girls had gathered enough wood they bound it in bundles with grass ropes, bundles just large enough to carry on their heads. Then they would bring it all to Tsananapa. They would put the bundles in a row in front of her, and she could choose the bundle that her heart desired.

Always they did this, the girls of the village of that chief.

But one day girls of another village came to the mother of this child and begged her to let Tsananapa go with them to gather wood. First she refused, but they kept on begging, begging, begging until the mother agreed. Then they went to the mountains, where the wood is dry and black.

They walked, they walked, they walked, until they came to the place where the wood was. Then they said Tsananapa must sit down on the ground.

But she said: "*Aaaa!* How can I sit on the ground? The dust will make my body dirty!"

But they reminded her that she was not at home, but in the mountains now.

So she sat in the dust, and her little dog sat beside her. The girls left their food there and went into the bush. They walked underneath the trees, they walked round the corner of the mountain, and when they had gone a long distance they made plans to kill Tsananapa.

They said she was proud.

They said she thought she was better than they were.

They said that a person who had such an opinion of herself should be killed.

When they had gathered enough wood, they bound it together in bundles and went back to the place where Tsananapa and her little dog sat and waited.

When they came there, they saw that she had eaten some of their food. She had eaten, and she had given some to her little dog to eat. They were very angry about this. They grabbed her, Tsananapa. Some held her arms and others pinched her throat. They strangled her. They strangled her, strangled her. And when she was dead, they put her body in a crevasse in a rock. They rolled a big boulder in front of the crevasse, and then they went home.

That dog of Tsananapa's saw what they had done. He wept, he wept over his mistress. He wept, he wept *iii,iii,iii!* just as though he were very cold. He wept *iii!* and he did not want to leave the crevasse where the body of Tsananapa was.

The chief was at the *khotla*, the gathering of the men. When he came home he asked his wife where Tsananapa was, and his wife said that she had not yet returned from gathering wood.

It grew later. It grew late and the chief waited for his child, but she did not come. Then he sent his men to the other village to find out whether the girls had returned from gathering wood.

"Yes, the girl children are all home."

"Where is Tsananapa, who belongs to the chief?"

"*Chè*, she went to see her grandmother."

Now the chief sent a man who could run fast. He must go and search for Tsananapa at the home of her grandparents.

No, she was not there. The old people had not seen her.

They searched through the night. They searched the next day and they could not find her, Tsananapa, the darling of the chief and his people.

And while they were searching, the little dog came to the hut of the chief. He came alone, and he wept. He wept *iii,iii,iii!* just as though he were very cold.

"Where is Tsananapa?" they asked.

"In the crevasse where the girls put her," he replied.

"Why did they put her there?"

"Because she was dead. They strangled her."

Then the parents of that girl child wept bitterly. And the dog also wept over that child, *iii,iii,iii!* as though he were very cold.

They buried her.

Then the chief called the whole tribe together. A *pitso*, a gathering of the tribe, was to be held. No one dared to stay away. The old ones also had to come. The old ones and the sick ones also.

When the tribe was gathered together, the chief told them of the child that had been murdered. It was a sad story, and everybody wept, for everybody had loved the beautiful child of the house of their chief, loved the beautiful child with a great love. They wept with the parents, and the little dog wept *iii,iii,iii!* just as though he were very cold.

The chief waited for the verdict of the *pitso*. And when they spoke they said that the girls who had strangled Tsananapa must also be killed.

Chè, it was good. They killed those girl children, and the chief did not want them to be buried. They were not buried. They were not buried.

The year began, and the year ended, and the parents of Tsananapa still mourned over their child.

The second year also began and ended, and the parents of Tsananapa still mourned over their child.

Then the third year began and the third year ended, and still they mourned. They and the little dog.

And when the next year of mourning was over, it was four years that they had mourned over this child, they and the dog.

Ke tsomo ka mathetho, which means: this is a true tale of the Basotho people.

22. Masilo, Masilonyane, and the Old Woman

They, the old people, tell of two brothers. The first one was Masilo and the younger was Masilo-the-young: Masilonyane.

They went hunting.

They walked, walked, walked until they came to many ruins. It was a village long abandoned. The people had gone away, the walls of the houses had already fallen in, the corral walls lay flat over the heads of the many old people who had been put away there after they died.

It was at this deserted village that Masilo and Masilonyane arrived. There they parted. Masilo went where he went, and Masilonyane walked there where he walked.

And it was this one, Masilonyane, who saw the hand coming out between the loose stones of an old corral wall! The thin hand of a very old person.

Yo, it was a frightening thing, this! The hand that was so thin moved! *Yo*—of such a thing he had never heard! It was surely an old person who had been buried and now wanted to come out again. *Yo yo yo!* He called Masilo and told him about it. But his brother did not want to come near. Masilonyane took a good hold of the hand that stuck out between the stones and he pulled. He asked his brother to help him, but his brother refused. He refused.

So Masilonyane pulled alone. He pulled, he pulled, he pulled and, when the thing was out of the ground, he saw that it was a very old woman. She looked just like other women who are very old. Only the big toe of one foot was different. It was very big, and it looked like a piece of dead wood. Such a toe surprised Masilonyane, for he had never seen a toe like that.

The old one spoke to him and said: "Child of my child, it is you who pulled me out, and it will also be you who will have to carry me to other people. I am too old, and I cannot walk far."

Then Masilonyane bent down. The grandmother climbed onto his back and held him tightly round the neck so that she should not fall off. So he carried the old woman back to his village.

Masilo walked with him and was astonished because an old woman would *pêpa*, would ride on the back of a young man, and he was astonished to see such a big wooden toe, a big wooden toe such as he had never seen before.

When Masilonyane grew tired, he wanted his brother to help him carry the old woman. But Masilo would not, he merely laughed at his brother. He said it was not he who had pulled the grandmother out of her grave, so why should he *pêpa* her? *Bê!*

They walked farther. When they passed a thicket of bushes they saw a hartebeest standing there. He ran away when he saw the people, but he had given Masilonyane a plan. He said: "Grandmother, get down quickly so that I can kill that animal. I will skin him, and then I can use his skin to tie you to my back. It will be your *thari*, your carrying skin, and then it will not be necessary for you to hold so tightly round my neck."

She did so. She got down and sat on the ground and Masilonyane pretended to run after the animal.

But when the old one could not see him any more he quickly darted in another direction and hid from her, from the old one that he had to carry.

She waited, waited, waited. And when he did not come back, she got up and went to hunt for him. But she walked with difficulty, because she was stiff with age and because the toe on one foot was very heavy. She walked slowly, and as she walked she talked to herself. She said: "Here are the footprints of my child. Here the one foot trod, and there the other foot trod."

Then she walked along the footprints of Masilonyane until she came to the place where he was hiding from her. She climbed on his back again and clasped her arms tightly round his neck so that she should not fall off.

Masilonyane grew very tired. He called to his brother. He begged him to help him carry the old woman. But Masilo would not, he merely laughed at his brother who had to carry the old one with the big toe such a long way.

They walked, they walked, they walked until they came to a flock of wild ostriches.

"Grandmother," said Masilonyane, "climb down for a little while. I want to catch an ostrich for you. His legs are longer than mine, and he is stronger than I am. It will be better if he will *pêpa* you."

Then the old woman got down. She sat down on the ground and waited for the young man to catch an ostrich for her.

But, when he was a little distance away, he again ran off and hid. Again she walked after him and talked to herself: "The feet of my child trod here. Here the one foot trod, and there the other trod; here the one trod again, and there the other trod again."

So she walked along, walked along, until she came close to the hiding place of Masilonyane. When he saw the grandmother with the big toe approaching, he said to the ostriches: "Catch that old woman who is coming along, her with the toe. Eat her up. Eat her up altogether. Just leave the toe."

The ostriches caught her, that old woman. They killed her and ate her up. Ate her up altogether, only not the toe, the toe that looked like a piece of dead wood.

Then Masilonyane took his axe and split the toe open. When it was open an ox came out, a pinto ox that looked like a guinea fowl. *Ghillick*—he was beautiful, that ox! He had the name of the multi-colored fowl: it was Ghaka-'malane.

Behind Ghaka-'malane a whole herd came out of the toe. Much cattle: bulls and oxen and cows with their calves. They roared and walked behind the pinto ox to the village of Masilonyane.

When the big brother saw the new riches of the little brother he came to him. He even ran and said, "Give half of your cattle to me, brother of mine."

But Masilonyane said, "I refuse, as you refused when I begged you to help me."

But the big brother went on entreating him. He said: "You can keep the whole herd, only give me the pinto ox. My heart desires that ox."

Masilonyane refused to give him the ox. Then Masilo kept silent, but in his heart he was busy with an ugly plan. He began to complain of thirst. He said they should seek a well where they could drink water.

They searched until they found a well. Over the opening lay a heavy, flat stone. They lifted it up, and Masilo said: "You hold the stone, so that I can drink first. The thirst has nearly strangled me. After I have eased my thirst I shall hold the stone so that you might drink."

They did so.

Masilo drank first. Afterward he held the stone, and while Masilonyane was drinking he suddenly let go so that the stone hit Masilonyane, and his dead body fell into the water.

But they say that the heart of Masilonyane came out of his body. It became a bird. A pure white bird. And it went to sit on the horn of Ghaka-'malane. It rode on the horn of that pinto ox until they reached the village where the two men lived. And, as far as they went, the bird sang of the misdeed of Masilo. So he sang:

> *Tsoili, tsoili, tsoili,*
> Masilo has murdered Masilonyane by the well,
> His desire was to own Ghaka-'malane . . .

When he saw that all the people were listening to him, he told them that he, the white bird, was the heart of Masilonyane. He said they could go to the well and see, there they will find his blanket and his weapons, where he had left them behind with his body.

Then they believed him.

The chief was very angry when he heard of the murder. He called his people together. It was a big *pitso*, that gathering of all the people.

The little bird rode on the horn of Ghaka-'malane to the place where the chief and his councilors sat on blankets made of jackal skin to hear the case.

The heart of Masilonyane told them with its song what had happened: *tsoili, tsoili, tsoili.* He told them everything. Just so. *Yoalo.* All the people heard it. They believed what they heard and insisted on the death sentence for Masilo.

The chief gave the command that the head *induna* should chop Masilo's head off, right there in front of all the people. And he did so.

Then Masilo was dead. His heart was also dead. But the little white bird remained the master of the great herd of cattle. Every day he rode with them to the grazing ground, he rode on the horn of Ghaka-'malane.

And when the people saw it, they said: "No, that is he, that one! That is Masilonyane. It is only his body that was murdered. There is his heart, as white as the hail, riding every day on the horn of Ghaka-'malane, in front of our eyes."

And so the story of the old people comes to an end.

23. The Bride of Chief Bulane

There was once a chief who had only two daughters. He had no other children. He had only two daughters. The big one was stupid, and that was why they called her Sehole. But the father did not care that she was stupid, for he loved her very much. He loved her very much, because she was the first child of his house.

Now the other daughter, the little one, was very clever, but the father had no love for her. Only the dog loved her and hated the stupid one, not because she had no brains, but because she teased him so. She could not stop teasing him. That was why he hated her, and when she came near to him he always wanted to bite her.

The chief saw this and told the daughter of his heart to stay away from the dog. But her head was hard, and she would not listen. She kept on, kept on teasing the animal. When he lay quietly sleeping with his head on his paws, she would pull his tail or tickle his mouth with a straw pulled from the broomstick. And when he flew at her she would rush to her father and hide behind his back and laugh at the furious animal—*ya-ya-yaaaaaa-yaaaaaa!*

It made the hatred of the dog boil higher and higher. Every day it boiled higher, boiled higher, boiled higher. He would surely have bitten her to death long ago if his master had not always stopped him. When the big man went to the gathering of the men, the *khotla,* and the dog had to stay home with the womenfolk, he hid the dog in a hole he had dug inside the reed screen that was in front of the huts in which he and his family lived. Over the opening he laid a large flat stone. It was far too heavy for the dog to move if he should want to come out of the hole. And when the animal was in the hole the heart of the father was at peace, even when he was away from home. Then the mother took care of the stupid daughter, but, when she had to go and work on the lands or gather wood for the fire, the younger daughter, she who was so clever, took care of the stupid one. Because she was so clever they called her Hlajane, the little clever one.

Now, it happened that the chief went one day to the *khotla,* the gathering where men decide on matters of importance. And while he sat there on the ground with the other men, his wife went to gather dried dung for the fires, and the two daughters were alone at home: Sehole, the stupid one, and Hlajane, the clever little one.

The dog slept in the hole underneath the flat stone that he could not lift. It was there that he slept. And Sehole was quite safe, she sat outside in the sweet sunlight. She leaned against the reeds of the screen, and Hlajane did the work that her mother had told her to do: she swept, swept, swept the floor. She took the dirt out to throw it on the ash heap, but she always kept an eye on Sehole, to see whether she still sat quietly against the reeds of the sheltering screen, in the sweet sunlight.

When Hlajane wanted to go to the spring to dip water with the clay pot, she went to look again and saw the stupid one still sitting where she had sat all morning. She sat quite still, *tu-u-u-u,* she did not move, *tu-u-u-u.* She sat just like that. Just like that. *Yoalo. Yoalo.*

Then Hlajane went with an easy heart to the spring to get water.

But the stupid one had seen her go. As soon as the little one could be seen no longer, she stood up. She stood up and went quickly to the covered hole. She took the flat stone between her two hands and pushed it away from the hole. She pushed it far enough for her to get her head into the opening. She stuck her head into the opening. The dog growled with rage, and she laughed at him, *ya-yaaaaaa! ya-ya-yaaaaa!* Then the animal leaped up and grabbed her by that stupid head. He pulled it right off her body and ate it up. After he had eaten it up, *ffooo!* Hlajane came back from the spring and saw the body of her sister lying there, just the body without the head, and, when she saw that the hiding place of the dog was open, she knew what had happened. She thought first of her father. He would blame her, Hlajane, for the death of Sehole. And his anger would be very great. She was afraid of it.

Swiftly she pushed that flat stone over the opening again, so that the dog should stay inside and not do any more damage to the body of that stupid one, she who was already dead, she who was the beloved of her father the chief. Then Hlajane quickly, quickly threw a blanket over the body of her sister and went inside the hut to look for food to take with her, because she would have to flee before the fury of her father. She would have to flee, and without food one could not flee, and live. But when she came out of the hut with the food, she saw that her father had already returned. He sat on his haunches by the body of Sehole. He stroked the body of his beloved child and wept like a woman. And when he saw Hlajane, he looked at her in anger and asked: "*Ná*, how did this thing happen, *ná?*" but his voice was hard.

"It is the dog that did it, Father," she replied, and her voice was frightened, like the voice of a little bird when a hawk circles above it. "Sehole pushed the stone away while I was at the spring."

The blood shot into the eyes of the chief. His eyes looked the way they did when he drank too much beer, and he grabbed Hlajane with one hand. He pulled his lips back from his teeth like a leopard about to attack, and with a voice like that of a fierce bull he bellowed:

"Then I must have *your* head. I must have it for the body of Sehole. Your head is good, it is soft. If she too has such a head on her body she will also be clever like you and the other girls of the tribe."

As he spoke, he pulled his hunting knife from his belt. With it the head of Hlajane was to be hacked off, to go to the body of the firstborn child, to the body of Sehole, the stupid one.

But just as the knife touched the throat of Hlajane, she changed. She changed into a wind, a little whirlwind, that slipped out of his hands and kept on whirling around, whirling around, whirling around through the door of the reed screen so that he could not catch her. It whirled around the yard, it whirled between the huts, farther and farther away, farther, farther, farther! It plowed over the ash heaps of the village, it whirled by the spring, farther, farther, farther . . . round the corner of the mountain until it disappeared completely, until the father could not see the whirlwind that was his daughter any more.

Then he went again and sat by the body of his dead child, and he wept with a loud voice. He wept so loudly that the dog heard him and wept with him.

"*Whow-wow-wow!*" wept the dog. "*Who-o-o-ow! Who-o-ow!*"

It gave the father a plan, a very good plan. He lifted the heavy stone from the hole and called to the dog to come out. He called nicely, nicely, nicely! He called nicely, so that the dog should not be afraid, and, when the dog stood in front of him, he talked to him. He said:

"You are the murderer of the firstborn of my house. Now you have to be sentenced to death. But I am the chief, and I will spare your life on one condition: you must fetch for me the head of Hlajane. I want it for the body of Sehole. Then my child will live again, and she will be as clever as the owner of that head. You must take the spoor of Hlajane. It is not the spoor of a human, it is the spoor of a whirlwind. Here in the shelter of the reed screen your nose will find the scent, and you must follow it, follow it, follow it to the place where the whirlwind again took the form of a girl. If you bring that head to me, you will not be killed as a murderer."

The dog looked deep into the eyes of the chief, he wagged his tail and let his nose slide over the ground until he picked up the scent of his beloved mistress, and away he went. He followed the spoor that the whirlwind had left behind, out by the door of the reed screen, over the yard, between the huts . . . farther, farther, farther . . . over the ash heaps of the village, by the spring . . . farther, farther, farther . . . round the corner of the mountain, until the chief could not see him any more either.

And with his nose to the ground the dog went until he reached another place, there where Bulane reigned. And it was there that he found Hlajane. She sat by a spring and she held a cracked clay pot that she had found in the reeds, and with it she dipped water to drink.

The dog did not rip off her head as the cruel chief had told him to do. No, he went to lie at her feet, he looked deep into her eyes until she spoke to him and laid her hand on his head. Then he wagged his tail to and fro, to and fro, to and fro, and he shut his eyes and he went to sleep.

Hlajane felt comforted, for now she was not alone any more in this strange country. She felt safe, because the dog of their house was there to protect her.

That night the dog took the cracked clay pot that had been lying among the reeds. He took the clay pot and turned it upside down over his mistress, so that she should be covered in the darkness of the night. And he himself went to lie down beside the clay pot, to protect her from the man-eating animals that prowl around at night and come to the drinking places to slake their thirst.

So Hlajane slept. She was quite safe until the dark became light enough for another day. And when the women of the village of the young chief Bulane came to the water hole with their clay pots they found Hlajane in the clay pot. The broken clay pot. But she lay like one dead. *Tu-u-u-u.* And the dog hid in the reeds so that he could see what would happen.

The owner of the cracked clay pot went to pick it up and fill it, but she could not lift it at all. *Yo!* It was a curious business! The other women came to help her, but they could not move the pot either. It was too heavy, far too heavy. And then they decided that the clay pot was bewitched. No, it could not be so heavy without being bewitched. It could not. They ran away from the danger, back to the village to tell their menfolk about this matter. "Great evil awaits at the spring, in a cracked clay pot," they said. Then came Bulane, the chief, the most fearless of all the men of the tribe, and he went to the spring. Behind him walked his foreman, the *tuna*, and four stalwart men of the tribe who did not want their chief to face the danger alone.

When they came to the spring they saw that broken clay pot. But it was not lying on its mouth any more. *Yo*, it was an ugly thing! Now it was up straight! It sat as a clay pot should sit, with its mouth at the top! *Mè*, mother mine, this was something that could not be explained. What was going on? They were astounded!

Now they saw something else: little footprints running away from the pot. They were the footprints that the feet of a young girl would make in the sand. In every sandy spot they saw the little footprints, in every sandy spot right to the side of the creek.

Bulane and his men followed those little footprints. Inside the creek bed they saw the footprints of a dog alongside the footprints of the girl. The men put their own feet right on the footprints, on all those footprints all along the canyon, right to the top of the canyon, and there they found the girl and the dog.

She, Hlajane, sat on a flat stone in the bed of the creek. Her little feet had grown tired from walking such a long way, and she soaked them in the water below the stone, and behind her sat the dog. But the dog kept his eye on Bulane and his men as they crept nearer to them. The hairs on his neck stood up straight and he growled, so that they should know he would fly at them if they did any harm to his mistress. His growls, and the long fangs he showed to the strangers, made them stand quite still.

When Hlajane saw the young chief she lowered her eyes, and with her hands she dipped water from the stream and poured it slowly over her feet, the feet that had grown so tired from walking so far.

Mè oe, she was beautiful! Never in his life had Bulane seen such a beautiful girl! Among all the young girls of his village, and all the young girls of neighboring villages that he had seen dancing at the song festivals, he had never seen one who was beautiful enough to become the wife of the chief. That was why he had not yet taken a wife.

But now his eyes had seen Hlajane, and he loved her immediately, there where she sat by the stream, scooping up the water and letting it flow over her feet. No, he loved her very much, with a love that was red.

"I greet you, *murato*, beloved! Peace!"

She greeted him also, but kept her eyes lowered. She rubbed the sole of her foot against the rough stone. And with her hand she dipped water from the stream and trickled it slowly over the foot that she rubbed, rubbed, rubbed against the stone.

"My men!" said he. And they replied, "*Morena!*"

Then he spoke further: "This one is the woman I have chosen. Go and tell it to my parents. It will make glad their hearts that have already grown old. And bring me a big fat ox so that we can slit its throat for this young woman. It will be to her a token of my love."

They did according to the words of the chief. They brought the ox, they slit its throat, and they built big fires so that they could cook the meat. From the hand of the chief Hlajane received a piece of the cooked meat. It was a tender piece from the inside of the thigh, which they had roasted over hot embers. She received it with both her hands held out together, side by side, and the heart of Bulane was full of joy when he saw this, for he knew it was a sign that she loved him also.

The dog also got some of the meat, but it was Bulane himself who held out the meat to the dog. He ate it, and his heart grew white for this unknown chief who was courting his mistress in such a dignified and worthy manner. He walked at the heels of the young chief when he carried the big piece of fleecy white stomach fat to Hlajane, the piece of stomach fat that looked like fluffy white clouds against the sky, when he held it up for her to see.

"Make out of this a robe for your hips, mother of mine," said Bulane, addressing her in terms of great respect. The girl politely held the palms of her hands out next to each other to receive the fat. And she spread it on the flat rock so that the wind could dry it. And when the wind had dried it she folded it neatly round her hips and secured it with her girdle of beads. And then she was even more beautiful than before. *Yo,* she was beautiful! She shone, so beautiful was she. That Hlajane.

The old mother of the chief was very glad when she heard of the things that were happening in that canyon. But it did not become her as the mother of the young man to go and speak to the girl. So she showed her pleasure in the ways she had learned from the old people, in the ways of her tribe.

She slaughtered a sheep for the chosen one of her son. She took the gall bladder, and, after she had squeezed the green liquid from it, she rinsed it with clean water from her clay pot. She rinsed it, she rinsed it, she rinsed it, and when it was clean she blew it up until it was round and lovely. And she sent it to the young bride together with the meat of the sheep. She sent the stomach fat also, after she had dried it in the wind.

Hlajane was very glad about the gifts. She was very glad. She tied the gall bladder in her hair and hung the stomach fat around her shoulders. The little curls of the stomach fleece lay on her brown shoulders like soft white clouds against the evening sky.

Yo, then she was beautiful! Even more beautiful than before.

But her beauty was too great, for it made the light of the sun grow dim. Then Bulane took her in that dusk that surrounded them and led her to his village, to the hut that his mother had built for her daughter-in-law, long even before they knew of Hlajane. And when this beautiful girl was inside the hut, the sun again shone as brightly as before.

In that hut Hlajane stayed until the day came that the tribe gathered for the wedding feast of their chief.

The people of Bulane unrolled grass mats and spread them around the hut of Hlajane, until the ground was altogether covered by the mats. Then the young people clapped hands and sang. And then Hlajane was led out of the hut by the old women of the village. She wore her wedding robe, the skin of an ox, and round her throat was a broad, shiny band that was a gift from the old chief, he who was the father of Bulane.

But when she came out of the hut a frightening thing happened. Again her beauty dimmed the light of the sun. It became dark round the people. It was black as the blackest night. The clapping of the hands ceased and the young people stopped singing, everybody wailed aloud over the evil darkness. But the old women knew what had to be done. "Quickly take the shiny band from your neck, mother," they said to the bride, "and hit the ground with it."

Hlajane heard them, and she did so. She took that shiny ornament from her neck and hit the ground with it. And, as she hit the earth, the light came back into the sun and it fell brightly and strongly again on the beauty of the bride of Bulane.

The whole tribe rejoiced when they beheld her beauty, and everyone was glad that the chief had at last taken a woman who could bring heirs to their royal house.

Thus was the wedding of Hlajane and Bulane. And in due time the news went from one mouth to the other that the wife of the chief would get a child. Then the women of the tribe began counting the moons with her, as they appeared in the sky. As many moons have to be counted as there are fingers on a person's two hands, if one finger has been broken off. So many moons it was that they counted.

One moon followed the other. It grew and died as the one before, and after it there came a new one. Every new moon, every new moon they counted until the number of nine moons had been seen in the sky, and then they knew that the time had come that the chief would see his first child.

But it did not happen. The child did not come. Another moon had already appeared in the sky . . . it swelled and then it shrank, but still the firstborn of the *lapa* of the chief stayed away.

Ghillick! This was an ugly thing! *Hm!*

The old women talked about this matter among themselves. The young woman needed their help again. She needed it. They brewed medicine from the right kinds of leaves and roots and went to give it to Hlajane to drink, but it did not bring the child. They did as their elders had told them to do: with their headscarves, with branches of trees, the women beat the walls of the hut in which the expectant one was, but it did not help. And then the people of the tribe knew where the trouble lay. When that tenth month was nearly dead, the old men went to talk with the chief. The one who walked in front was the one who let the snake come out of its hole.

"*Morena*," they addressed their chief, "that child of yours who is letting us all wait, wait, wait has a reason. He has a strong reason, and it is we old men who are sent to make it known to you."

"Open your heart, Father. I will listen. What is the reason?"

"The reason is this, *Morena*. That child is a proud man. He is the son of a chief. And his mother is also the daughter of a chief. How can the child be born now, *Morena*, and bring dishonor to his mother? He cannot do it. He knows that his father did not do right to his mother. Can he appear before his father rectifies his mistake?"

"Father, those are hard words I am hearing now!" spoke Bulane. "Tell me how I did not treat that wife of mine in a way that is right? Did not my mother build for her the most beautiful hut in the whole village? See her clothes! Is there another woman who dresses as well as she? Tell me what other woman wears such a long *karos*, such a long blanket made of jackal skin? Speak, Fathers!"

"No, it is not the hut or the clothes, *Morena*," replied the old men. "It is the matter of cattle! Chief of ours, have you taken oxen and sheep from your herds and sent them to the father of Hlajane, as is proper for a wedding? *Ná?* Tell us and we shall know. We shall know, *Morena*."

"*Chè*, Fathers, that I did not do. The chief who is the father of Hlajane wanted to kill her."

"That is no matter. He exchanged her mother for cattle, from her father. The children of that woman are his possessions. How can you take his daughter for yourself without paying for her, without compensating him for working so many years while he was raising his daughter for you? It is a wrong business. Your child, that child who cannot be born, is telling this to you. He will not show himself until right has been done to his mother. You will see, *Morena*."

"*Chè*, Father, your words are wise words. I did not do right. I made a mistake, and I am willing to send the cattle away. But now I have not one person in my village who knows how to walk to the village that is the home of my wife's people."

"*Whow-o-ow!*" the dog wept from the hut of Hlajane.

Then the old men said: "The dog knows the way, *Morena*. It is not he who should take the cattle? When that debt of honor has been paid, Grandfather Bulane, then your child will be born."

The chief took this wise advice to heart. And it was forty of his best cattle and thirty of his fattest sheep that he counted out of his herds to pay for his wife. The forty oxen and the thirty sheep he sent, together with the riding horse that was to take care of the sheep, to the father of Hlajane, and it was the dog who chased them to the village of Hlajane's father.

And only when the cattle and the sheep had been gone for a day was the boy child of Bulane born. After the dog had brought the cattle and the sheep and their herder the horse to the village of the father of Hlajane, he quickly turned round and ran back to the *lapa* of the young mother. He went into the maternity hut and lay down by the feet of his mistress, there where she lay sleeping on the grass mat with her little one beside her. And here is the end of the story.

APPENDIX:

1. *Index of Motifs*
2. *Index of Tale Types*
3. *Comparable African Folktales*

[The following comparative data have been kindly supplied by Mr. John M. Vlach at the behest of the Editor. The type and motif numbers are, of course, from the Thompson indexes (see the list of references below). A plus sign (+) following a motif number indicates not so much a proposed new motif but rather a slight change or refinement in an already extant motif that makes that motif a more accurate description of its occurrence in these tales.]

References

Kenneth W. Clarke, "A Motif-Index of the Folktales of Culture Area V, West Africa," Ph.D. thesis, Indiana University, 1958.

Mona Fikry, "Wa: A Case Study of Social Values and Social Tensions as Reflected in the Oral Traditions of the Wala of Northern Ghana," Ph.D. thesis, Indiana University, 1969.

May Augusta Klipple, "African Folktales with Foreign Analogues," Ph.D. thesis, Indiana University, 1938.

Stith Thompson, *The Types of the Folktale*, Helsinki, 1964.

——, *Motif Index of Folk-Literature*, 6 vols., Bloomington, Indiana, 1955–1958.

Index of Motifs

A. *Mythological Motifs* *Tale Number*

A2281.2.+ Hen loses hawk's needle: enmity between them . 5
A2426.2.8 Why dove coos 7
A2433.6.1.1 Why the turtle lives in the stream 7
A2494.13.10.3 Enmity between hawk and hen 5

B. *Animals*

B11 Dragon 18
B15.7.10 Animal unusual as to skin 18
B81.0.2 Woman from underwater world 11
B131.1 Bird reveals murder 22
B192 Magic animal killed 1
B221 Animal kingdom 14, 19
B221.1.+ Kingdom of baboons 19
B240.4 Lion as king of animals 14
B263 War between groups of animals 19
B301.1.+ Faithful animal mourns master's death 21
B411 Helpful cow 11
B421 Helpful dog 10, 23
B450 Helpful bird 1
B524.1.1 Dogs kill attacking cannibal 6, 20
B524.1.2 Dogs rescue fleeing master from tree refuge . . . 20
B531 Animals provide food for men 11
B563 Animals direct man on journey 10
B575 Animal as constant attendant of man 21, 23
B604.1 Marriage to snake 10
B620.1 Daughter promised to animal suitor 9
B622.1 Serpent as wooer 9
B646.1 Marriage to person in snake form 10

C. *Tabu*

C331 Tabu: looking back 4
C644.+ The one forbidden thing: returning to bride's home
  country after marrying 19

D. *Magic*

D281.1.1 Transformation: man to whirlwind 23

Tale Number

D421 Transformation: mammal (wild) to object 14
D672 Obstacle flight 18
D721 Disenchantment by removing skin 10
D721.3 Disenchantment by destroying skin 9
D801.1 Magic objects possessed by witch, sorcerer, or evil
dwarf. 12
D1031.0.1 Manna 3
D1208 Magic whip 12
D1221 Magic trumpet 4
D1364.23 Song causes magic sleep 12
D1421.5.1.+ Magic horn calls monster to capture fugitives . 17
D1470.2.1 Provisions received from magic tree 15
D1546.1 Magic object controls sun 23
D1860 Magic beautification 3

E. *The Dead*

E613 Reincarnation as a bird 22

F. *Marvels*

F451.5.1 Helpful dwarfs 15
F525 Person with half a body 17
F551.+ Remarkable foot when split open yields cattle . . . 22
F571.3.+ Very old woman with large wooden toe 22
F954 Dumb person brought to speak 1
F969.7 Famine 3, 11

G. *Ogres*

G11.6 Man-eating woman 6, 20
G30 Person becomes cannibal 6
G61.1 Child recognizes relative's flesh when it is served to be
eaten 14
G84 Fee-fi-fo-fum 6, 18
G88.+ Cannibal has long nail 20
G269.10 Witch punishes person who incurs her ill will . . 12
G312.2.+ Spirit-man in rock devours men and cattle . . . 15
G346 Devastating monster 6, 20

H. *Tests*   *Tale Number*

H210 Test of guilt or innocence 8

J. *The Wise and the Foolish*

J1421 Peace among the animals 16

K. *Deceptions*

K521.2.2 Disguise by mutilation so as to escape 14
K550 Escape by false plea 13
K553.1 "Let me catch you better game" 6
K606.1 Escape by playing music 9
K827.1 Fox persuades bird to show how she acts in storm . . 13
K851 Deceptive game: burning each other 14
K931 Sham nurse kills enemy's children 14
K1241 Trickster rides dupe horseback 2
K1241.1 Trickster rides dupe a-courting 2
K1818 Disguise as sick man 2
K1911 The false bride 4
K1911.3 Reinstatement of true bride 4
K1911.3.3 False bride fails when husband tests her 4
K2155.1.+ Mud smeared on innocent person brings accusa-
tion as accomplice to escape 14

L. *Reversal of Fortune*

L52 Abused youngest daughter 20, 23
L61 Clever youngest daughter 23
L162 Lowly heroine marries prince 3, 4, 20

N. *Chance and Fate*

N271.4 Murder discovered through knowledge of bird's language 22
N825.3 Old woman helper 10, 15

P. *Society*

P251.2 Two brothers 22
P252.1 Two sisters 1, 23
P253.0.2 One sister and two brothers 18

Q. *Rewards and Punishments*   *Tale Number*

Q41 Politeness rewarded 10
Q41.2.+ Reward for scratching loathsome person 10
Q211.4 Murder of children punished 21
Q211.9 Fratricide punished 22
Q280 Unkindness punished 3
Q415 Punishment: being eaten by animals 15

R. *Captives and Fugitives*

R11 Abduction by monster 12
R17 Abduction by whirlwind 17
R231 Obstacle flight—Atalanta type 9
R251 Flight on a tree, which ogre tries to cut down . . . 20
R311 Tree refuge 20

S. *Unnatural Cruelty*

S12 Cruel mother 3
S12.6 Cruel mother refuses children food 3
S73.1 Fratricide 22
S113 Murder by strangling 21
S411.3.+ Barren cow banished 11

T. *Sex*

T548.1 Child born in answer to prayer 3
T554 Woman gives birth to animal 9
T574 Long pregnancy 23

W. *Traits of Character*

W181 Jealousy 1

INDEX OF TALE TYPES*

Animal Tales

37 Fox as Nursemaid for Bear 14

* Most of these types could properly be listed as motifs. However, the episodic structure of Basotho folktales gives a special prominence to certain motifs, allowing them to be considered as tale types. Hence, tale number 13 is composed of two related tales and tale number 14 has type 37 as part of its narrative.

Tale Number

56D Fox Asks Bird what She Does when Wind Blows . . . 13
62 Peace among Animals—the Fox and the Cock 16
72 Rabbit Rides Fox A-courting 2
122 The Wolf Loses his Prey 13
122D "Let me Catch you Better Game" 6

Ordinary Folktales

425A The Monster (Animal) as Bridegroom 9, 10
781 The Princess Who Murdered Her Child 22

COMPARABLE AFRICAN FOLKTALES

Tale Types

Type 37

[Fikry] Wala; [Klipple] Zulu 3, Kaffir, Basuto, Venda 2, Rozwi, Jindwe, Ndau, Mashona, Tonga, Ila, Lamba, Northern Rhodesia, Nyanja, Tambuka-Kananga, Larusa, Chaga, Massi, Nyoro, Ganda, Ndongo-Ovambo, Congo 3, Kuba, Ewe.

Type 62

[Klipple] Ndau, Nama-Hottentot, Egyptian Sudan, Soninke.

Type 72

[Klipple] Xhosa, Nyanja, Mbundu, Yoruba, Nupe.

Type 122

[Thompson] Africa (general).

Type 122D

[Thompson] Kaffir, Basuto .

Type 425A

[Klipple] (under type 425) Basuto 2, Zulu, Hausa 2.

Type 781

[Thompson] Africa 12; [Klipple] Southwest Africa, Basuto 3, Bantu, Yao, Kinga, Mbundu.

Motifs

A2426.2.8 [Klipple] Mbundu.
A2494.13.10.3 [Thompson] Cameroon.
B131.1 [Thompson] Ekoi, Zulu, Tonga, Basuto.
B221 [Clarke] Agni 2, Gold Coast 5.
B240.4 [Clarke] Togo, Dahomey.

B421 [Clarke] Togo 3, Ashanti 3, Yoruba, Ikom 2, Ekoi, Temne, Gola; [Thompson] Zulu 2, Basuto 3, Kaffir 2, Benga, Angola.

B450 [Clarke] Ibo 3, Togo, Yoruba, Vai, Nigeria 4, Ashanti, Ekoi, Agni, Gola, Slave Coast 2, Ewe; [Thompson] Benga, Angola, Kaffir 3, Swahili, Basuto.

B524.1.1 [Clarke] Ikom 2, Ashanti, Ekoi, Temne, Gola; [Thompson] Basuto, Zulu, Kaffir.

B524.1.2 [Klipple] Basuto 2.

B531 [Clarke] Nigeria; [Thompson] Angola.

B563 [Thompson] Benga, Basuto 3, Ekoi; [Fikry] Wala 6.

B620.1 [Thompson] Angola.

B646.1 [Thompson] Zulu 2, Kaffir, Basuto 2.

C331 [Thompson] Fang 2, Africa (general).

D281.1.1 [Clarke] Togo; [Thompson] Basuto.

D672 [Clarke] Gold Coast 2, Togo, Mende, Gola; [Thompson] Duala, Basuto 2, Mpongwe, Kaffir, Africa (general) 2.

D721 [Thompson] Pangwe, Africa (general) 2.

D1208 [Clarke] Yoruba, Mende 2, Ashanti.

D1221 [Thompson] Ekoi.

D1470.2.1 [Thompson] Zulu.

D1860 [Thompson] Fjort, Hottentot.

F451.5.1 [Clarke] West Africa 2.

F525 [Clarke] Liberia; [Thompson] Africa (general) 2, Basuto, Zulu, Luba.

G61.1 [Clarke] Ashanti 2, Togo 2, Ewe; [Thompson] Angola 2, Kaffir, Basuto.

G84 [Thompson] Africa (general), Kaffir 4, Zanzibar, Ekoi 2, Basuto 4, Angola, Zulu.

G88 [Thompson] Angola.

K521.2.2 [Thompson] Basuto.

K553.1 [Thompson] Kaffir, Basuto.

K606.1.1 [Clarke] West Africa (general).

K827.1 [Klipple] Xhosa; [Thompson] Basuto, Hottentot.

K851 [Klipple] Lunda; [Thompson] Kaffir, Ila, Basuto 2, Tonga, Zulu.

K931 [Clarke] Agni, West Africa (general); [Thompson] Basuto, Ila, Kaffir, Benga.

K1241 [Clarke] Tiv, Liberia, Yoruba, Nigeria, West Africa (general); [Thompson] Africa (general), Nigeria, Angola.

K1241.1 [Thompson] Nupe, Africa (general), Yoruba, Nyanja, Mbundu, Xhosa.

K1911 [Thompson] Africa (general), Zulu, Kaffir, Bushman.

K1911.3.3 [Thompson] Zulu 2, Angola.

K2155.1 [Thompson] Ila.

L52 [Thompson] Basuto.

L61 [Thompson] Kaffir.

N825.3 [Thompson] Africa (general), Ekoi 4, Basuto 4, Kaffir 3, Zanzibar, Angola 3, Zulu.

Q41 [Clarke] Slave Coast, Gold Coast.

Q41.2 [Clarke] West Africa (general), Ashanti, Ekoi, Agni, Kpelle; [Thompson] Chaga, Alo, Batanga, Bulu, Bamabara, Hausa.

Q211.4 [Clarke] Ashanti, Kpelle.

Q211.9 [Clarke] Slave Coast.

Q280 [Clarke] Ibo 2, Nigeria, Togo, Ashanti 2, Ekoi, Temne; [Thompson] Duala, Bula, Congo 2.

Q415 [Clarke] West Africa (general), Slave Coast, Vai, Liberia, Togo, Kpelle.

R11 [Clarke] West Africa (general).

R17 [Thompson] Basuto.

R231 [Clarke] West Africa (general) 2, Togo, Yoruba, Ashanti; [Klipple] Betsimisaraka; [Thompson] Gold Coast, Zulu, Angola, Kaffir, Yoruba.

R251 [Thompson] Togo.

R311 [Thompson] Zulu; [Clarke] Ibo, Slave Coast.

S12 [Thompson] Basuto 3, Angola.

S73.1 [Clarke] Slave Coast, Mende 2.

T554 [Thompson] Zulu 2, Kaffir.

T574 [Thompson] Madagascar.

REGISTER BY TALE IN THIS COLLECTION

Tale no. 1
  Motifs: B192; B450; F954; P252.1; W181.
Tale no. 2
  Type: 72.
  Motifs: K1241; K1241.1; K1818.
Tale no. 3
  Motifs: D1031.0.1; D1860; F969.7; L162; Q280; S12; S12.6; T548.1.

Tale no. 4
  Motifs: C331; D1221; K1911; K1911.3; K1911.3.3; L162.
Tale no. 5
  Motifs: A2281.2.+; A2494.13.10.3.
Tale no. 6
  Type: 122D.
  Motifs: B524.1.1; G11.6; G30; G84; G346; K553.1.
Tale no. 7
  Motifs: A2426.2.8; A2433.6.1.1.
Tale no. 8
  Motif: H210.
Tale no. 9
  Type: 425A.
  Motifs: B620.1; B622.1; D721.3; K606.1; R231; T554.
Tale no. 10
  Type: 425A.
  Motifs: B421; B563; B604.1; B646.1; D721; N825.3; Q41; Q41.2.+.
Tale no. 11
  Motifs: B81.0.2; B411; B531; F969.7; S411.3.+
Tale no. 12
  Motifs: D801.1; D1208; D1364.23; G269.10; R11.
Tale no. 13
  Types: 56D and 122.
  Motifs: K550; K827.1.
Tale no. 14
  Type: 37.
  Motifs: B221; B240.4; D421; G61.1; K521.2.2; K851; K931; K2155.1.+.
Tale no. 15
  Motifs: D1470.2.1; F451.5.1; G312.2.+; N825.3; Q415.
Tale no. 16
  Type: 62.
  Motif: J1421.
Tale no. 17
  Motifs: D1421.5.1.+; F525; R17.
Tale no. 18
  Motifs: B11; B15.7.10; D672; G84; P253.0.2.
Tale no. 19
  Motifs: B221; B221.1.+; B263; C644.+.

Tale no. 20
    Motifs: B524.1.1; B524.1.2; G11.6; G88.+; G346; L52; L162; R251; R311.

Tale no. 21
    Motifs: B301.1.+; B575; Q211.4; S113.

Tale no. 22
    Type: 781.
    Motifs: B131.1; E613; F551.+; F571.3.+; N271.4; P251.2; Q211.9; S73.1.

Tale no. 23
    Motifs: B421; D281.1.1; D1546.1; L52; L61; T574; P252.1.

BIBLIOGRAPHY

Arbousset, Thomas. *Relation d'un Voyage d'Exploration au Nord Est de la Colonie du Cap de Bon Esperance*. Paris, 1842.

Beguin, Eugene. *Les La-Rotse*. Lausanne, 1903.

Bleek, W. H. I. *A Brief Account of Bushman Folk Lore*. London and Cape Town, 1875.

———. *Reynard the Fox in South Africa, or Hottentot Fables and Tales*. London: Trübner, 1864.

———. *Zulu Legends*. Pretoria: J. L. van Schaik, 1952.

———, and L. L. Lloyd. *The Mantis and His Friends: Bushman Folklore*. Cape Town: Maskew Miller, 1923.

Bourhill, E. J., and J. B. Drake. *Fairy Tales from South Africa*. London: MacMillan, 1908.

Bourke, M. *Badoli the Ox*. Cape Town: Howard B. Timmins, [1949?].

Brincker, Peter Heinrich. *Fabeln & Märchen der Ovambo-Herero*. Leipzig, 1886.

Brownlee, F. *Lion and Jackal with Other Nature Folktales from South Africa*. London: Allen & Unwin, 1938.

Callaway, H. *Nursery Tales, Traditions and Histories of the Zulus*. Springvale: John A. Blair, 1868; also Kraus reprint, 1970.

Casalis, Eugene. *Etudes sur la Langue Se-Chuana*. Paris, 1841.

———. *Les Bassoutos*. Paris, 1859.

Erasmus, P. F. *Legendes uit die Skemeruur*. Johannesburg: Afrikaanse Pers-Boekhandel, 1960.

————. *Towerbeelde by die Aandvuur*. Johannesburg: Afrikaanse Pers-Boekhandel, 1957.

Hertslet, J. *Bantu Folk Tales*. Cape Town: African Bookman, 1946.

————. *Endulo: Magic Tales from Africa*. Pietermaritzburg: Shuter & Shooter, 1940.

Hoffman, C. A. *Bantoe-stories uit Transvaal*. Cape Town: Nasionale Pers, 1938.

Jacottet, E. *Contes et Legendes des Basothos*. Paris: Revue des Traditions Populaires, 1888–1890.

————. *Contes Populaires des Bassoutos Afrique de Sud; Recueillés et Traduits*. Paris: Ernest Leroux, 1895.

————. *Litsomo 1, Litsomo 2, retold*. Morija, Lesotho: Morija Book Depot, 1930, 1941.

————. *The Treasury of Ba-suto Lore*. Morija, Lesotho: Morija Book Depot, 1908.

Keyser, A. *Venda-sprokies*. Johannesburg: Voortrekker-Pers, 1949.

Kidd, D. *The Bull of the Kraal and the Heavenly Maidens: A Tale of Black Children*. London: A. & C. Black, 1908.

Lestrade, G. P. *Some Venda Folk-Tales*. Cape Town, University. School of African Studies. Communications. New Series, no. 6 (1942).

McPherson, E. L. *Native Fairy Tales of South Africa*. London: Harrap, 1919.

————. *Wonder Tales of South Africa*. Cape Town: Unie-Volkspers, 1941.

Maingard, L. F. *Korana Folktales*. Johannesburg: Witwatersrand University Press, 1962.

Markowitz, A. *With Uplifted Tongue: Stories, Myths and Fables of the South African Bushmen*. Central News Agency, South Africa, [1956?].

Martin, Minnie. *Basutoland, Its Legends and Customs*. London, 1903.

————. *The Sun Chief: Legends of Basutoland*. Durban: Knox, 1943.

Metelerkamp, S. *Outa Karel's Stories: S. A. Folk-Lore Tales*. London: MacMillan, 1914.

Murgatroyd, M. *Tales from the Kraals*. Cape Town: Howard Timmins, 1968.

Ndawo, H. M. *Inxenye Yentsomi Zase Zweni*. Mariannhill: Mission Press, 1920.

Oosthuysen, H. *Sprokies uit Pondoland*. Johannesburg: Afrikaanse Pers-Boekhandel, 1952.

Postma, Minnie. *Bulane*. Pretoria: Van Schaik, 1952.

———. *Legendes uit Basoetoeland*. Johannesburg: Afrikaanse Pers Beperk, 1954.

———. *Legendes uit die Misrook*. Johannesburg: Afrikaanse Pers Beperk, 1950.

———. *Litsomo*. Johannesburg: Afrikaanse Pers Beperk, 1964.

———. *Ons Maak die Kleipot oop*. South African Broadcasting Corporation, 1968.

Potgieter, E. F. *Enkele Volksverhale van die Ndzundza van Transvaal*. Pretoria: University of South Africa, 1958.

Reynolds, R. Liguori. *Tales of the Blue Mountain*. Johannesburg: Afrikaanse Pers-Boekhandel, 1965.

———. *Whispering in the Reeds: S. A. Folk Tales and Legends*. Johannesburg: Afrikaanse Pers-Boekhandel, 1964.

Savory, P. *Basuto Fireside Tales*. Cape Town: Howard Timmins, 1962.

———. *Bechuana Fireside Tales*. Cape Town: Howard Timmins, 1965.

———. *Xhosa Fireside Tales*. Cape Town: Howard Timmins, 1963.

———. *Zulu Fireside Tales*. Cape Town: Howard Timmins, 1961.

Schoeman, P. J. *Vulindaba*. Cape Town: Nasionale Boekhandel, 1964.

Sekese, Azariele. *Me Khoa Le Maele a Basotho*. Morija, Lesotho: Morija Book Depot, 1962.

Sicard, H. von. *Ngoma Lungundu: eine Afrikanische Bundeslade*. Uppsala, Sweden: Almquist & Wiksells Boktryckeri, 1952.

Slattery, Hand B. *Makulu und andere Südafrikanische Neger-Märchen*. Zurich: Artemis-Verlag, 1954.

Smith, C. W. *Beyote and the Bull with Other Folk Tales from the Transkei*. Durban: Knox, 1947.

Sprokies uit Noord-Transvaal. Johannesburg: Afrikaanse Pers-Boekhandel, 1956.

Theal, G. M. *Kaffir Folk-Lore*. London: W. Swan Sonnenschein, 1882; also Kraus reprint, 1970.

Thomas, E. W. *Bushman Stories*. Cape Town: Oxford University Press, 1950.

Waters, M. N. *Cameos from the Kraal*. Lovedale, South Africa: Lovedale Institution Press, n.d.

[This bibliography received major assistance from Anna H. Smith, Librarian of the City of Johannesburg and of the Strange Collection of Africana.]